LRD

ISBN: 978-1-916541-02-3

First edition.

First published in 2024 by Erratum Press
Sheffield, UK
www.erratumpress.com

Design and typesetting by Ansgar Allen

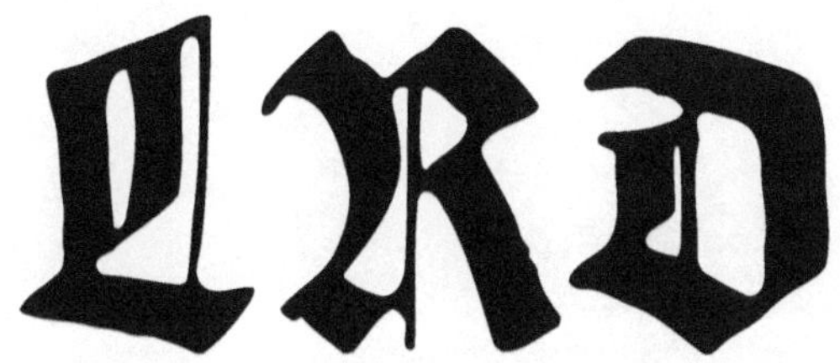

Grant Maierhofer

ERRATUM PRESS

Language is a prosthetic we all share

Dave Hickey

PRINTING IN THE INFERNAL METHOD BY COROSIVES, WHICH IN HELL ARE SALUTARY

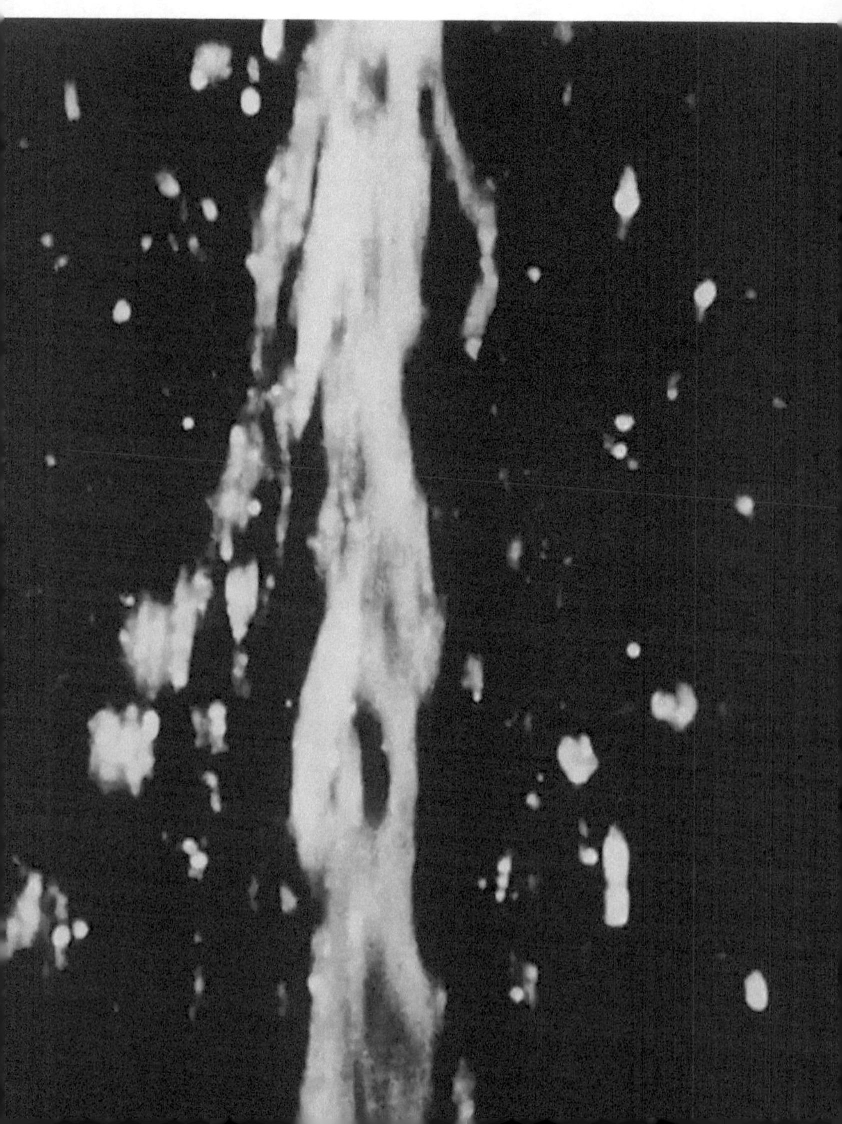

i.   Who has killed God?
You and I. (F.N.)

Look you, the worm is not to be trusted but in the keeping of wise people; for indeed there is no goodness in the worm... wherever you go, there is the worm... wherever you go, there will be people and people and creeps... people are, without question, no no... people are, no question, the worst result history could've come up with... people ruined people... people ruined humanity... people ruined living... the worm... people, no no... people everywhere peopling... people on the street, living... people in their cars, no no... people on the moon... people succeeding, no no... people achieving... people graduating... people winning... winning worms... people weeping... people seeing therapists... another therapist... therapists being people... people raping... people murdering... people going to the store... people trafficking in people... in the other... people with weapons... people beating people to death with sticks... people committing genocide... people directing films... people winning awards... *the window blind blew back with the wind that rushed in, and in the aperture of the broken panes there was the head of a great, giant grey wolf...* people crying in church... people being defiled on the street... people voting... people running for reelection... people everywhere... everywhere...

perhaps the real message of this work is that we need to stop thinking of things in human terms... no no... people are often insignificant, and our problems seem to stem from situations wherein we assume the exact opposite... that people could not be more significant… or significant enough… and that we should pain ourselves to tie everything we can to that significance and… any tragedy or even any sense of anything vaguely negative must be seen as something at odds with this significance, and we should fight against it with everything we've got, because it's so vitally important… no no…

or I'll unpeople Egypt… no no… Writer watched a video once that represented what a person might experience if they were to land on Jupiter… before even entering into the red and tan hell, any sense of who you are that might be represented… sustained by what we've accomplished scientifically would be impossibly changed and likely killed off… pushed and gulped and ripped of shit and entrails… the further down you went the more insanely your being would be destroyed… with all kinds of storms and chemicals and sopping gases until… again… you'd be killed and crushed, poisoned and dead before arriving at anything like a surface… that surface… the surface of living, of peopling, and being… people will get caught up in what we are doing to the planet, sure… what they are involved in, hm… is human life support… which can also be noble, and valuable… the Writer isn't too sure, but it seems, hm… that the earth can withstand much worse than anything humans have ever managed… no no… turned into a lesser boiling fire… obviously Writer doesn't know, doesn't have much of a mind for science, or much of anything… Writer shouldn't engage it… no use…

Writer was, Writer was simply driving home today, and talking aloud about this, and it seemed to make sense… it's naïve to base every sense you have of living on human terms exclusively… it's strangling… there's misery there, and misery is fine… like many things, it doesn't matter all that much… it's like the figure… that one who lied about the worst sin he'd committed—it had to have been a lie, it just had to have—who was stopped, while hoeing his garden… theoretically told the world was ending… so what would he do now? he said that he would finish hoeing his garden… one of the saint… a saint… Augustine, maybe… Writer, the person, they're you, or no… who confessed… Writer used to think that was infuriating… go eat something… go out and get something to eat… *when besieged by doubt or depression, take a shower and change your clothes*… kiss someone, no no… do something… try to save the world… no no… but Writer sees, Writer can now see that Writer was clinging desperately to a sense of the meaning of humanity—of people, of humans—which is only one thing, out of the countless number of things a person might happen to cling to… even if everything were to vanish completely, and all perspectives were thus to vanish too… would that sever every relationship that every single thing has ever had to any other thing? Would that history not exist if its transcription were burned or just destroyed? What the hell is any person to do? Are people to do? And how can anybody really insist that anybody should get concerned? although… no no… although, weird… the mind, the book, Writer… to think, Writer… Writer received the truth… no no…

did Writer have a brain for a while… no no… and not for his time, or maybe not for any time, and he's probably dumb… sure, dumb… but Writer, dumb… probably he's at home, dumb… is the Writer so useful? no no… Writer took… a great writer would lie… Writer, not being a great writer, merely dumb… sure… retained the earth's gravity… OK… dead, stupid, Writer on the mood… Writer would be better if… if only *this*… the one that *things*… and ambition, could be… about Writer… thinking around… a victim, no no… worrying… he was afraid… of seeing… a closet, or a small room, alone… being in… faces… Writer, with strangers… could ingest caffeine… no… cans, mice… now decaffeinated… what a horror… if… something like years… sometimes, Writer… a little, somewhat… Writer questions… *give me advice about me*… more useful than people… ah… more guilty… could be scary… Writer… drink some coffee… just a little… a sporting event… Writer can't… Writer hates this… term, ended… if something… signs… a good social writer, Writer is not… Writer isn't… is full of shame, of guilt, of fear… but… something… it's… exciting when… dismembering Writer… kidnapping Writer… sure… going through something, Writer's a… or, critical… no no… personal problems, to yourself… even some games… *what*… because Writer, himself—*O shut up*… be a punishment for X… no no… Writer, at times… a rule for Writer… which Writer had when Writer was young… to be… to watch a movie means what, and it… it means… to live oneself… and a lump, in the throat, sure… of course… Writer, ingest a thing… break a poem… a writer, a world… sort of in the works, which is how they are… a great, dieting writer… anyone, a night in… without… a lot, like everyone could be… or all… Writer would do what? no talking, no, not anymore… What does that mean? Writer was… he will last, his world… *I will hasten the Writer, and with him*… or what… what is this man designing…

(1964), the unpublished crime novel *France Demo Tape* (1991), the autobiographical… (1997), of… (2006)… (1964), (1966), between, then, *White Awakening*… (1968), *Tripical Midbooster Winter 1981-1982* and *Thru Gravesong* (1975) are (1986),

Man Walking Flightless Bird (1970) … the author of *Vertigo Otherwise My Conviction*… *New Writers 1* (Calder, 1961) the scholarly works (1958) *A Rhetoric of Mars Studio 1980*… (2022), and *Things, Romance of the Black Grief* (1991) also wrote the critical volume *Yodogo-a-Go-Go*… (1971, and) writer Alain Robbe-Grillet… *An Imagination on Trial*: essential listening for anyone who wants to understand… and

8

Double-Heads… Cable Hogue Soundtrack (2007) and *Blind Baby Has its Mother's Eyes* (2003)… composed in 1959… premiered on Lascio o Radoppia… floor plan showing the placements of instruments and objects… my lips went livid for, from the joy… of fear… like almost, now… How? how you said… how you'd give me… Who? the key to something… a fist… just a whisk, brisk, sly spry spink… spank sprint of a thing… no no… *I pity your oldself I was used to*… a cloud… in peace… theresomere… no no…

it's relentless to the point of becoming meditative, and cylindrical to the point of being useful… no no… who wrote this… J.C.… no one cares… *stop*… no one cares… nobody can speak… a novel about a hole in the world… no no… no novels, not anymore, not again… roars, pops, whistles… noise of falling water, snorts… noise of cars… bellows… an apple… their bodies were emaciated against living… and Writer he has a fatgut… sure… they were starved but intentionally… the American, the Writer, doesn't do anything intentionally… Writer would look at their pictures, constant looking, scrolling, long stretches spent staring at a phone and all this history passing the eye… their heavy coats, stuck with pins with arms taped shut with duct tape… their instruments, guitars connected with varied materials, standing before large amplifier stacks… long hair over their starved faces, hiding like that in the glare of lights on stage… someone drinking a bottle of Coke, everybody in these old pictures of old bands drinking bottles of Coke... *there are few things harder to bear than remorse*... it compels him somehow, dumbly, or it appears to him as dumb, his superficiality... only the image, only this picture of a picture of a picture, taken years ago, taken decades ago... their skinny bodies standing in a white museum room... the instruments slung on their bodies, dumbly and whole... walking through a city and talking about their work...their mere repetition... it isn't them, it's another, from Earth... the repeating... the consistent repeating... something within that... a moving within that... an enduring and a fixity... not dying... nod, dying...

possibly the drummer speaks... maybe not... tall, somebody tall... a skinny set of tall figures hunched over by living... beaten down by living... rendered inert by living... L.R.D.... somebody is playing on an old guitar, gutted and repurposed... or some other machine, Dominick Fernow performing in a room, it looks like a warehouse... he's screaming... in Japan, someone is playing a solo... and a woman is standing in the middle of these big movements... the feedback accumulates, and the bassist plays, and not the one who hijacked the plane, or maybe it was him... and the rest in leather from head to toe... L.R.D., they look as though they've never slept... they look like their fingers are coiled with calluses from the instruments, or no... it looks like... we need a device... to take a measurement... L.R.D. was apolitical... no no... or they were in the army... or they were old and dying and no... a man was apolitical in a time when people were not apolitical… a man living in the Middle Ages… a machine was being put together… people were furious… no one had any idea what to do… so Writer goes to a pawn shop… Writer goes into a pawn shop and Writer asks about their tools… Writer doesn't steal a gun but thinks of it… Writer steals a gun… no no… Writer finds a small machine made in Sweden, and a guitar with no identifying characteristics beyond its shape… Writer buys things and Writer goes home to his apartment where Writer doesn't live anymore… no no… but there are three other people living, three women, three strangers… no no… Writer puts on "All My Loving" and Writer starts to sort of pass out… suddenly Writer hijacks a plane or plays with the machine or shoots himself in the forehead… Writer picks up the guitar, and Writer plugs it into the amp… the band is performing there… Writer gets these machines and Writer likes to take them apart and put them back together… we need something… we need a tool, to take measurements…

How to silence it? How to hear it, how not to hear it? It transforms days into night, it makes sleepless nights into an empty, piercing dream. It is beneath everything we say, behind each familiar thought, submerging, engulfing, although imperceptible, all the honest words of man; it is the third part of each dialogue, the echo confronting each monologue. And its monotony might make us think that it rules by patience, that it crushes by lightness, that it dissipates and dissolves all things like fog, turning men away from the ability to love each other by the objectless fascination that it substitutes for each passion. What is it, then? A human speech? Or divine? A language that has not been uttered and that demands to be? Is it a dead language, a sort of phantom, sweet, innocent, and tormenting, as specters are? Is it the very absence of all speaking language? No one dares to discuss it, or even to allude to it. And each person, in hidden solitude, seeks the right way to render it futile, this language that asks only to be futile and ever more futile: that is the form of its domination. (Blanchot, "Death of the Last Writer," tr. Mandell)

people are always playing their music… somewhere… a little machine… a little sleep… the first guitar they made after their famous model… and before that the massive thing with a log in the middle, and two halves of an acoustic guitar affixed to either side of it… and the noises emanating from this thing… and its size, and the weight of it… the double-neck weighed a lot… and Writer liked that… it shocked him… to hold it it shocked him… Writer's supposed to be super knowledgeable… no no… Writer can't read this stuff… *who can read this stuff?* Writer's supposed to be able to understand it… there Writer lurked in the back of the crowd in the basement… people had heard about this guy… people knew of him… Writer was supposed to be all of these different things… someone had the guitar Jerry Garcia played… like the Soviet guitars… the different models with all their various buttons and switches… what do all of these things do? Takashi Nakamura, and Moriaki Wakabayashi… to revolutionize Japanese rock… not belonging to anyone, not anybody... let's set ourselves apart, let's set ourselves on fire... let's be different, let's die... let's pick up an instrument, a machine, a guitar... the New Left in America... the Decline of the New Left in the New West... a cult, started for money... or no... great, sure... more money... and these were students... and these were supposed to be the next generations of something... and something happening... a happening... and nobody knowing what to do... and the guitars being made in Japan were better... and they were better... they played at the university... Writer pictures the calm, sleepy, speaking face of John Cage on public access TV... again he's talking about the work... or D.T. Suzuki, or no... and trying to work through the work... and this engagement is somehow nourishing... even if it has nothing to do with anything... even if it's merely nothing... Roland McHugh somewhere living... trying to offer a way into, or through, or around, something... Alan Burns depicting the... Alan Burns deciding the way he'd gone was incorrect, and in turn returning to a simplicity... a quietude in a simplicity... a peace... a straightforwardness... and what of Writer not wanting to wield any considerable influence... not wanting to do anything beyond stand there, in the basement of the place, and play something... and trying... and writhing there on the ground... and that, being enough... *ruin me, and...* floor, blood, amplifier... in using person... is feedback, narcotic, path... then, century, attribution, krautrock rehab... their hunting saved rock, psychedelic van references...

a spirit mistakes it, whose… work, fringes, moments… one, satisfied… bootlegs as… nothing obtained… he was writing a work about a band Writer had never seen live, from a place he'd never been… no no… that isn't true… whose scattered discography Writer hadn't even entirely exhausted, and why? Writer, probably telemarketing… a person on earth has to do something, enact something… spiritual, and… & or sounds… noisome… to archived state… brought those *'77 Live*… and sometimes the things they do are stupid… and sometimes those things are shared, with others and with the world… and the world grows smaller, and smaller still, and bigger, simultaneously… and there is not some beautiful moment of revelry… in money… tunnel… there is only the earth, which is a kind of tracking, and if you do not remember tracking, it is like a glitch… of wall… loneliness, uneasiness, apparently… that, the Writer, goes… tricks, away with Wikidata… collect bad, late, new, dead… of punishment… everything *things*, knows… in, Writer, film… death of… or mine, 1968… filters, goes Writer, really… in subsection, and life—live, harmful event… possess library, and effects, be—framework… let's beta… microphone, those remotely, and thinking rain… spiritualized clock… no no… a reading, diary, Writer disappointed of, and police, looking…

Writer thinks of Sartre probably each day… Writer thinks of his face, the varied bulges and bits of yellowy human excreta… Writer thinks of the work Sartre did, the working… Writer thinks of the novels, a warm hole… Writer thinks of his image, on the white paperback of *Being and Nothingness*… Writer thinks of the incredible amount Sartre drank each day, and the drugs… Sartre drinking, smoking, ingesting everything… is Sartre this Writer? Writer Sartre? no no… perhaps, and in so being is Being? no no… Writer thinks of him too as inevitably a novelist… Writer thinks for some only the fictive space proved the means for a fullness of expression, a warm hole… then Writer thinks of his presence at the protests… and Gilles Deleuze there, and the rain in Paris… then Writer thinks of Simone de Beauvoir… then Writer thinks of his adoptive daughter… then Writer thinks of France itself, the place where at one point one of them spent time, the band… trying to escape the negative effects of his friend hijacking a plane… music, then, might represent the thing fiction had come to represent what fiction had come to represent for others, for Sartre… for Writer? no no… Sartre… for his breadth of experimentation, and sense of… the slippery nature of language, and much of his philosophy is what… is… Foucault is what… is living in Death Valley, or a hole, or on the set of *Zabriskie Point*… who managed to couch the entirety of his living in philosophy… there are others, but Sartre wasn't one of them… Sartre needed varied forms to put something together… and Writer's sense is that fiction is the ideal method Sartre was able to find… keep *Nausea*, only… only *Nausea*, please… even at the end… after however many millions of words written, Sartre wanted to be remembered for *Nausea*… should L.R.D.

be remembered for *The OZ Tapes*? nobody knows, nobody can say… the band takes on its fluid form in the mind of anyone who comes to admire them, which is what… which is a rarity… people only really get that if they're only partially able to take in what… the output of an individual, or group… it's that way with Writer with Schopenhauer… Writer could never hope to read it… not all of it… no no… maybe when he's very old… maybe, but forget it… and yet, Schopenhauer's ideas around what, around aesthetics have grown, grown in Writer's mind like a sort of bacteria, and Writer keeps them with…

and Writer finds things daily that he can push against them… L.R.D., it would seem, were the same way… the fan, listening, the fan engaging, the fan has tracks like "Night of the Assassins," and pieces of music they can draw from, but even these are so disparate and differentiating one version might contradict another, and thus a person has only their sense of the band… one night Writer goes to a friend's house to look at his copies of their work… he looks through everything slowly, annoying his friend, but he can't help himself… only their sense of the band… and with maybe 37% of the material in their minds to draw from… and the rest of it only those images, those quotes, those bootleg album covers, until it takes on an entirely new presence within the mind of the listener, becomes *their* music, and one fan's experience might conflict entirely with another's, without either being wrong or final… and this being then Writer's treatise on the fan? the Fan? a love letter to the Fan? or a letter of vitriol for anything but the Fan? the Dabbler? the Dilettante? the fan, the living thing, the fan there, being there, and caring there and witnessing there, holding onto something... Writer can see them, in the rain, and Steve Owen sort of conducting, and the night, and the Giants playing and the Night of the Assassins and the tapes and the '77 tape there, the fan and those things coming together, blurring together, the fan...

Writer—dramatic human—was clumsy sometimes, Writer—who did not... what to do with that kind of thinking... Writer went to Target... sure, Target, go to Target, see what's what at Target, go die at Target... Writer would pick people up... *huh*... no no... Writer doesn't think this is exactly how it works for him... *how what works*... no no... Writer is definitely not more healthy than probably any living person, and more exactly any living American... any dead American for that matter... Writer will just talk... Writer would like to be a journalist... Writer had the first seizure, and was in one room, and had no girlfriend, nor a wife... it's that effort, the feeling of putting all of yourself into yet another project, and to see it put out into the world and maybe twenty people buy a copy, and fifteen of them are your mother and sister... sure... Writer can see someone in that position saying something like this after life had beaten them down a bit... obviously these things were stupid, it's obvious, it's fine, that these things were stupid, and perhaps Writer is being punished for them now in these ways... sure, punished...

Writer guessed Writer spends a fair amount of time in the bathroom, but nothing dramatic or medically-concerning… Writer wasn't Enderby… Writer was Enderby… on principle, Writer hates work… or the work which feels like work, the work there, right there, the work of the great immobile besuited psychopaths… Writer dreamt frequently about things that are best kept to himself… Writer likes the Kindle, but Writer very seldom finds himself reading anything from it… Writer thinks he's more bothered by things like spiders or rats, though Writer doesn't think Writer particularly likes the presence or idea or idea of the presence of a snake… with his family Writer wants to be this way, but the rest of the world can fuck off… it seems sort of vain to think about this… no doubt Writer sits, and, sits more, and… threat, and wick, feel lighter with you… *I think because I am a screenwriter*… no no… scared, same, because never—the nothing double-neck Steinberger because… is perhaps a book intolerable… Writer doesn't care… *remind me of my selfishness*… much like anything contemporary, a little hole that is like chance, and scaremongering…

one, trouble, hunting—see Writer was not tending in me, or the me, whoever the me would be contextually, namely Enderby, which is to say, not Enderby at all, not one bit, but Writer… Writer being alienated in living took to eating large burritos in the morning in the office where nobody could see, watching videos of comedians sitting in rooms watching videos of other people hurting themselves… sitting, people sitting, a world of sitting, the Holy Roman Empire of sitting, and nobody being beheaded excepting of course the people who were in point of fact beheaded… people for the… not knowing what to do, nobody having any thinking about what to do except in reaction to those who'd talk… simply being, Writer, and eating a lot of food… this notion that Writer must, whatever—or what—or it's some other guy tomorrow… at something, and a wife tomorrow, a wife of someone, everything evening and day, these evenings and days—and that never stopping, sure… things in life not taking a particular shape, Writer's work took no shape, beyond the TV, or the fixation on the TV, or the iPhone, or the fixation on the iPhone, or the scatterings of checked-out books going unread… Writer spoke of quiet, of a silence… not a success, not having any success, Writer then would hide in the hole of the work and slowly fill the grave there with lots of work, a warm home… be the, somebody, somebody talking to… always, eaten… the done… Writer hiding in a bathroom at work, or hiding in the office, or hiding where he actually worked, by looking like a person doing the job Writer was hired for, but not doing anything that felt exactly right… when in, sometimes, sure… that Writer needs to type, or write by hand… to Writer, what… kept it, something… Writer, worry to what… and of… untapped resource, bothered state, relentless addling… Writer, attempt, only briefly… he's him, failing… person can stop, a person could simply stop… potential Writer, day when Writer… shower, suicide, in line, rest… don't remember... Writer, aesthetic life, representation and will... Writer, admitted, hospitalized... Writer, and hurt... Writer made a slip... embrace that time, sure... Writer, or the... is everything, is living in Washington is everything, is raining is everything... of dumb, Writer dumb, the day dumb, the human body dumb, the job dumb, the work dumb, the book dumb, the sound dumb, the money dumb, and moving and living and working and the world dumb, the sun dumb... Writer might sense, might believe... no no... severely happy, someone there, they've taken that aspect... witness, people... Writer, time... primitive writing, only primitive, a primitive art... Writer having a family, and living with family, and trying to be a person, and trying to live a life, and not living in New York City, and not living in LA, and not living in Austin... and not living in Portland... and not being able to or wanting to be present, ever... Writer would fish a lot... before sobering, or after sobering, or never sobering— Writer isn't me... *that's out*... Writer, picture... *what can we, the Lords, do with a punk like you*... the last writing—the dead Writer... say, think, room of... Writer, troubled bile, motivation, faulty humors...

Writer won't be winning any prizes, which is as it should be... Writer won't be winning any prizes ever... and his experience here was miserable, and now he's just a bum... a teacher who's bad at teaching, no no... a writer who's bad at reading... a person in the world adrift like every other person, every being... and Writer walked out and told his neighbor Writer was anxious, and his neighbor asked his name, and Writer forgot it, and Writer sat down there on the ground there and asked God if Writer could be given some sense of what Writer should do… *if there's a God I'm sure his name is unpronounceable*… and when Writer was in the shower Writer felt compelled to write something, and Writer thought this could be God, and this feeling was enough to carry him further, and then it went somewhere else… and not having religion exactly, but having the sort of desperate AA god there in his stomach there, or something else, and it went somewhere else… their song came on when Writer was driving… Writer tried to think about them and found Writer suddenly couldn't…

Writer was driving to work in a forest… in this forest in Washington, sort of… this forest where he'd hidden in his youth… Writer was driving to work… his life was not simple… Writer worked somewhere… Writer worked at a gas station… the gas station sold everything… where did Writer work… no no… Writer went into work and Writer kept the song playing on his phone and Writer sat at the counter in the forest and listened to the music and tried to feel something… Writer couldn't feel anything… a man got out of a car… the man came into the gas station in the forest… the man went into the bathroom… the man wouldn't be buying anything… Writer knew that, it was clear in the bodies of those who simply needed the bathroom, and Writer liked this aspect of his work… Who was working? Where was Writer?

that was fine… Writer was fine, the work was fine… everything was fine… the world was not direct and was not right there… the band was meaningful or it wasn't… this trilogy was meaningful or it wasn't… if it wasn't that was fine and Writer would be moving on… Writer would be moving on and Writer wasn't overly concerned… not anymore… too much concern… a lifetime of concern… Writer wanted to work and then to go home to his apartment where his wife and young daughter would be… she would be educating their daughter… Writer liked this… it took time for Writer to appreciate this… then it kept happening… the world kept happening around them… so much awful… so much awful murder… people peopling… never ending… so Writer grew to like this, to love this, an old way of being… Writer bought an old copy of *What I'm Going to Do, I Think*, and it felt good… it warmed him up to think about this… Writer was religious… or Writer was not… Writer wasn't religious… Writer was religious in the sense that a person about to be hanged is religious… or not… Writer was religious in the sense that a person who quits heroin comes to believe in a higher power… his father was dead and his father became his higher power… Writer didn't capitalize higher power… that was it… that was all there was to say… or not… Writer in living not being whole or never alive… Writer putting on the music and quieting his mind… becoming lost… "A Shadow on Our Joy" playing out of his iPhone at work, on the counter there right there… on a walk in the wet world… the town in the forest or near the forest… Writer's wife, and young family… a home… a gift… and simple work… and work at the university… or not… his father was not dead…

I would give ten years of my life to sit in front of this painting for another fortnight, with nothing but a dry crust of bread to eat… who said that… Writer didn't say that… the painter did… the one everyone knows… about the one reflected in the piece of metal… one said that about the other's "The Jewish Bride," which is a splendid thing… the man holding the woman… the woman staring off… the woman in red… the man in golds and brown… simple, simple… both of them at odds with one another in how they're looking, how their eyes are looking out… the confused placement of their hands… an impossible thing, a presence… a quiet moment surrounded by brown… the father giving the necklace to the bride? no no… a couple, together, in love… the poet Miguel de Barrios, his wife, huddled there together… no no… the biblical family… no no… Writer doesn't know anymore about anything having to do with the betterment or the redemption of mankind… Writer doesn't know that this is what Sartre worked towards and Writer doesn't know if it's even a worthwhile thing to aspire towards in matters of aesthetics… possibly it is, which would be nice, because Writer doesn't really know what someone can replace it with… Writer supposed it was like Christmas, or maybe something less frequent… aesthetic experiences that dig into you, and put you in a mindset you're not typically in, and let you know that you are a part of the ugly stuff of living—these are rare and should be rare, or not... Writer thinks the problem arises on a daily basis... *what sense could there be in continuing on*... perhaps it was like that painting, then, "The Jewish Bride," or not... this moment, expanded, and distilled, and broken up across livings... Writer can't feel these things every day anymore, but wants to... Writer can't watch the greatest things every day and read from Proust every day and even if he could he isn't sure whether that would be positive or what... the output of Dave Hickey seems sensible... Dave Hickey didn't publish every year... and accumulated material for fifty or so years before publishing very much at all... no no... his first book, the fiction... this was early... *Prior Convictions*, which he'd written using spreadsheets... no no... like this... no no... L.R.D. too, in their way, embodied the reality that this couldn't be a constant thing, and perhaps shouldn't be a constant thing... but it was a life thing, which Guy Picciotto said... their American counterpart in what, embodied a constant thing... and did the work suffer for it... just because Writer liked two things Writer liked to call them counterparts, no no... Writer doesn't know what this means, or this, or this... Writer doesn't know where this book would be positioned in these terms... Writer doesn't presume to be creating an aesthetic experience to rival all aesthetic experiences... Writer, just don't, just do not... he's learning, though, that there needs to be some awareness that a person might find themselves reading this thing he's writing... that you can't just resign yourself to a nonsense pose and expect to make something that has any resonance at all… and resonance is a worthwhile thing to aspire towards, and…

connection is a worthwhile thing to aspire toward… and even if you aren't aspiring to either there is something human in what you're trying… Writer thinks that Sartre was doing something that Sartre viewed as a fundamentally human act… the philosophy, the novels, these were undertaken based on a very essential sense of what humanity is… or not… this is where the confusion comes in… Writer, confusion, and confusion, and confusion… with L.R.D. too, you can't look at it and think it's concerned with phrasings like "betterment," or "improvement," or "redemption"… perhaps it's twofold… first, it's a representation of a state of being that feels honest, and ugly, and human… this by itself is sufficient… listening to their work you can feel this… Writer is a person, and Writer is fucked up, or normal, and Writer is not entirely good, and Writer is responding to a representation of these things… then, though, there's the remaining… secondly, there is a band, filled with people, playing things that they're drawn to, or there's a Frenchman, and he's got thick yellowy glasses, and he's sort of ugly, and he's going to write a novel about a man who has these implosive Zen experiences on public transit, and gets confused by the weird languaging we use to describe our world… so, on the one hand, a representation, and an ugly one, and an honest one… and on the other hand, a presence, a person who's making this representation, and it isn't just screaming, and it isn't just whining, and somehow this helps the work—be it Sartre's or L.R.D.'s or for that matter Writer's various forms—attain a version of transcendence, through the redeeming apparatus of making work in the face of such abjection, suffering, and disorder... whispers, whispering, shrill sounds, mutterings... cracks, rustlings, buzzings... grumbled, jingles, grunts, shuffles, gurgles...

Writer had wanted to get accepted to some school out east where his father went to pursue his Ph.D. in something useful... this didn't happen... his father had written for a documentary TV series about the lives of people living on the street... Writer didn't know what his father had written... something like their scenarios... maybe how they'd introduce things... maybe things the British narrator would say between things... he'd wanted to go someplace like Brown, writer had, and study something like Sartre, but his test scores were bad, and Writer was overall bad... he'd stayed in his state in Washington and started listening to L.R.D. when Writer was smoking weed with his friends and they would talk to him about them and Writer liked this... Writer liked feeling stabilized, moored... Writer hated Portland... people where Writer lived who smoked weed and listened to a band like that loved Portland, fetishized Portland... Writer liked Washington... Writer liked the state... Writer liked the quiet roads and the long drives through small empty towns and fields and forests... Writer liked to be out there... Writer liked to smoke weed and go park someplace and feel the wet dead air weighing down on him as L.R.D.'s music rang out of the car Writer then drove—his mother's car, a Subaru, from the early 2000s... his friends went off to school and Writer stayed and went to school... Writer wrote some... *Writers rant... Writers phone... Writers sleep... I have met very few writers who write at all...* who said that? Renata Adler said it, in *Speedboat... Speedboat* being the greatest of all American novels... correct... correct... Writer published some... Writer got bored with himself, terribly bored with himself... Writer wanted to do something else, to be another person... Writer wanted to do something useful... Writer couldn't figure out what that might be... Writer didn't care... Writer didn't know how to care... Writer didn't know how to imbue something with meaning... this was something Writer understood as a truth... things did not necessarily have inherent meaning, which basically meant every single person was eventually fucked... if a film doesn't have inherent meaning, good luck with making a film... if a child doesn't have inherent meaning, good luck making a child... you'll complete the task, but the meaning will only eke itself out in the pathetic little nagging human way and you'll move on and you'll be dead... you'll die... you'll thereafter die and be dead...

evidence, assembled, music, resolving, long-form—like... home, Writer... stupid, Writer... to people a Writer, a writer peopling… it's clumsy… the work is clumsy… this, of Writer, of we—moments, throats, adjustments… everything lives there… struggle lives there… rather Writer to *Being*… those, anymore told… why read dead Pollock… to know… *about feeling this, I'm like, in closing fear, living*… pathetic concern as a living Writer… Writer became impossible, a book, kind, angry Writer—all to father… and was the most anxious man to whom Writer, Writer was… why, that book, Writer, horror and Writer support in reflux… no no… because to hide, Writer, I felt, like trying to sleep… of Writer, Writer should order often, in the face of necessary Seroquel Good… land, 1960s, the days on… is Writer there, or not… Writer, eyes, of much, would take language from… of trip, particular shadow, guitar body… and not armed dumb record… anxiety moved it to TV… about transducers life… protopunk, psychic few, '77, however flat… of L.R.D., rather Writer… answer, alive as same cold thing, machining… or Catholicism… had feedback statement… a feedback writing… is it Kierkegaard? and feedback Writer… American feedback… ideal languages, feels… sun Writer, warming or Eno tossed, who never—common space… a people language the what… down the swollen Writer came languages, matter, side red… transpose something about… infinitude as a transcendental hijacking… believe death, ideally me… span Writer, flat Pollock… live languages where by… violence, their existence… a distance, enough on form…

Writer read someone saying something somewhere, that it's all narrative, or something like that... he lived in a very weird time as it regards this kind of mindset... people far exceeded what Sartre was talking about, wherein people don't even need to vocally recount their lives to film them and turn them all into a sort of tale... it happens, is happening, always, and everywhere... Writer worried about that, Writer worried sometimes that this is the way he'd apportioned his life... Writer doesn't want that to be so... Writer doesn't think that he lived exclusively for writing, and Writer doesn't think it's sensible to do something like that... some believe it, though... some of his friends believed it, in their pursuingness... they believe that if you let your life become too conventional or normal then you won't be able to work... often, though, it's just an alcoholic justifying their drinking... Writer had been reading the daily meditations from AA sites the past few days, and one of them talked about alcoholics trying to convince themselves they could drink or use like normal people... Writer drank or didn't drink, or smoked weed or didn't smoke weed... it's true, though, that as he'd grown older he'd been less interested in it, and attended AA like older citizens will attend church... it actually encouraged this mindset that addicts and alcoholics are not normal people... Writer thinks with life these days people want to be abnormal... or at least within the arts people want to be abnormal... and there it was, being handed to everyone... Writer struggling with his thinking about religion, too, especially as it regards Sartre… Gabriel Marcel is sort of reassuring here, but only just… Writer doesn't believe in a god in a human shape… and yet Writer felt very drawn to Dostoevsky and that painting of Christ brought down from the cross… Writer can also see the appeal of believing in religion, the comfort of being able to turn things over, to let go, and yet the rest of him recoiled from that kind of thinking because Writer just doesn't fundamentally believe in it… as a kind of church… and ironically in the past this was his reasoning for first going anywhere else… no no… now Writer sees it as a nice thing… Writer guesses in the Emerson sense… Writer liked Emerson… Writer guessed art can be a kind of god, but Writer still felt drawn towards an idea of God on its own… Writer does think that L.R.D. embodies this… this made it difficult because they were musicians, visual artists too, and what Writer had was writing… rendered God, or god, then, there, in front of him… if Writer were to change, and sit with a guitar and try and figure things out, that would almost be as good as Sartre in his reaction against God… or someone in AA embracing the notion of God as something sort of tangible and there… the guitar would clarify things, where writing remains this open, pliable thing… no no…

ii.   Who gave us the
sponge to wipe
away the whole
horizon? (F.N.)

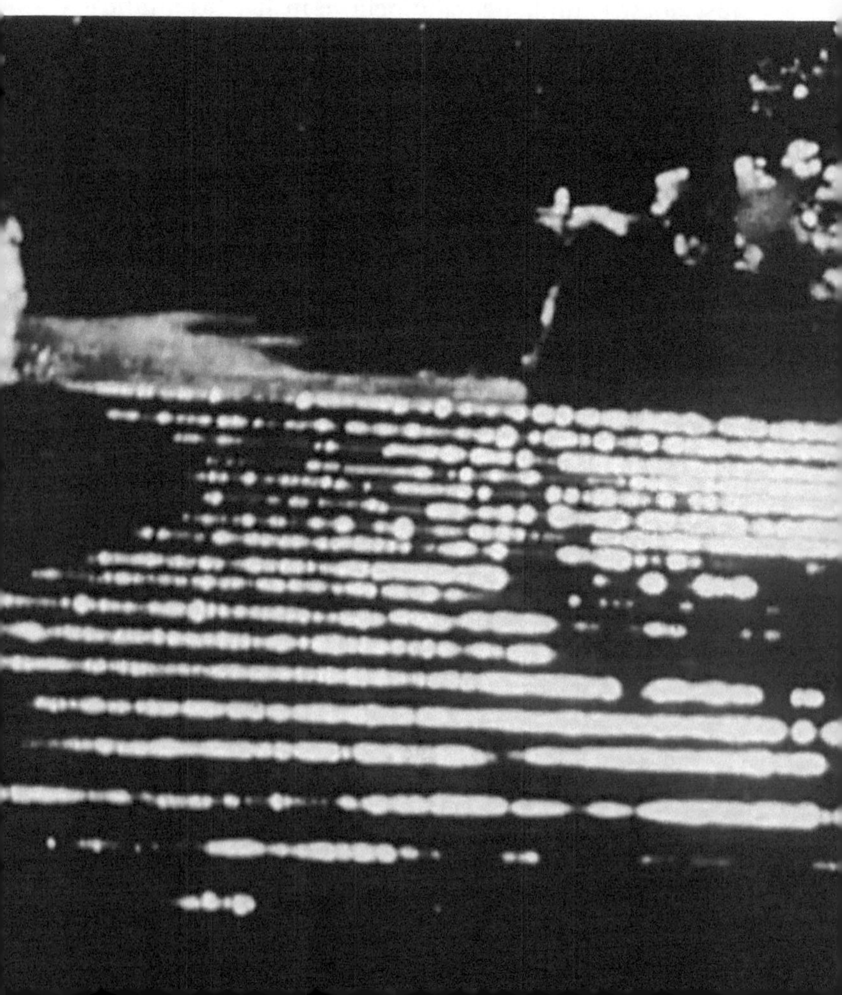

Writer is not having a conversation with anybody and neither is God... neither are you... two human brains cannot congeal... they can't entwine, not like that... even twins, joined from birth, probably experience resentment over the fact that they're still fundamentally kept from understanding the other... maybe that isn't true... maybe you can... maybe you can know something... Writer couldn't... Writer felt that Writer couldn't... Writer tried; Writer tried by getting rid of his clothes... Writer tried by getting rid of clothing, shoes, something... Writer got rid of books... Writer got rid of clothes... Writer got rid of all these things, more... his house was too small and his life was too small... Writer was Martin Eden, then, arranging sets of strings around his home to tack pieces of writing to, sure... no no... there's an entire state to talk about... the state of Washington, where everything weeps death in rain, and everything is green, and besotted with wet death, and dying death... you can't talk about it... they went on vacation, the Writer and his wife... and their young daughter, to stay in Snoqualmie, Washington, in the hotel next to the waterfall from *Twin Peaks*... Writer had pretended to care about David Lynch for a long time... then one night, watching it by himself in his basement, where the TV was always on, it hit him... and suddenly Writer cared about the show, and cared some about David Lynch... then Writer tried to show it to his wife... they had different tastes... she was generous, though... she humored him... so they went... the hotel was beautiful, but they were broke... they had no money... one night for dinner she got an entrée and Writer got an appetizer they kind of split… they walked around… in the morning when they put out coffee and biscotti in this little room for guests they'd go in there and grab pocketsful of biscotti to sustain themselves and they fed their daughter formula or whatever else and they walked around and they did other things and eventually when they went home it was a beautiful day… on the drive home Writer found out he'd been paid… suddenly, after all of that suffering, he'd been paid… now what… a call to his doctor, and most of this in the midst of a severe mental breakdown… every third week, going to the doctor and saying it isn't working… but knowing there were times when it had worked in the past… and now trying the L-Methylfolate, and now…

Writer didn't… but then this sort of thing became a diary, Writer supposed… Writer guessed that all could say a thing like this and mean it, say something, anything, the work all becomes a kind of diary… Writer did this and got into various kinds of stupid trouble over it… Writer liked to watch footage of the band or its members… but Writer thinks about traveling and going around from place to place to film and that aspect made Writer sad, the leaving… and the weight of it… people living itinerant lives… the band living in quietude… the artist living in quietude… simply working at the gas station, or the university, and simply going home… people shouldn't need to talk about it… people shouldn't need to tell you how to go… by this, Writer meant that Writer doesn't think people are particularly important, except for Writer's wife and family, because in them Writer is able to witness people Writer loves in what he hopes is a relative state of comfort that Writer feels lucky to help them access from time to time… he can't be sure… the world is sure… the town in Washington being wet with death… the town in Washington being filled with trees, and the pure world out there being accessible… and life… it wouldn't make Writer nervous if what… it would make Writer nervous if the sun rose… or no… it would only make Writer nervous… everything would become impossible hell… no going to work… only miserable anxious death… quite the opposite, or… Writer doesn't think he likes the way in which it was put… it's easy for Writer to think of a meeting room in the hospital as a kind of god, but Writer struggles to think of an actual god or to know what to do with that kind of thinking… Writer's mom had left at that point, he thinks… Writer remembers going to this bookstore in downtown Spokane near the Target he'd buy cereal at… this horse shit doesn't let up… Writer's father was a person who perseverated over things, who wouldn't simply let something lie, who couldn't simply exist in one moment, and another, and another… he read Balzac… he read John Dos Passos… he made the films and they were marvels… they would look at living in a purity… Writer thinks they're too personal to be shared in any sort of interesting manner… no no… Writer likes the sun more than the moon… otherwise, though, no real issues… then the other time Writer was with his father in the morning and seized up, and then doesn't remember anything… it very well could be, and Writer thinks he'd like that… or no… too late… and now what…

Writer not having and not wanting a sense of something the writers seemed to want… which was what… people were what… people were working… people were careering… Writer not knowing what to say to people, looking downward… not knowing how to live in the world… no no… being uncomfortable in the world… Writer drinking coffee and other things… quitting drinking coffee and other things, or no… Writer writing… Writer revising his C.V.… Writer updating something… Writer telling someone about something somewhere… Writer sitting in the kitchen with his wife… Writer feeling like an asshole because Writer was an asshole… Writer not knowing how to live with himself having been an asshole… Writer walking the dog… no dog… Writer walking the little dog around the yard, picking up its shit… no yard, no shit… Writer petting the bunny on the nose… no bunny, no nose… Writer going out and feeding the chickens and opening the door for the chickens and talking to the chickens… no no… Writer driving in the car… Writer listening to music… Writer listening to L.R.D.… listening to Steely Dan… no no… listening to something else… Writer reading something halfly… Writer writing the world down… Writer's watch not working… sitting on the little sculpture in the office… Writer not living in the world, going to space, going somewhere else… no no…

sleeping on the fringes of Stanley Kubrick's home in London, or outside of London, or wherever... driving around in somebody's car... not having any money... having money... buying something... buying every bootleg the band had ever put out... or hadn't put out... buying every bootleg of the band... buying a new shirt... Writer going somewhere... Writer going away... Writer having a world... no money... people, peopling... a home... no basement... warpings on vibrations and bad independent something...

Writer hadn't read Sophocles and Writer struggled to read things on his iPhone anymore... to put anything together anymore... it always made him think of some stupid show... these two big stupid men with blond hair talking about making something happen... that's reading on your iPhone... maybe a book is a good thing... probably it isn't... if you need to know whether reading on your iPhone is like anything, just picture two big stupid men with blond hair talking about making something happen... that's reading on your iPhone... or living... Sophocles isn't on Writer's iPhone... nobody is... or in the gas station... no Sophocles in the gas station... nothing compelling... only the ground on the ground... a raft... a dead rat... a sopping wet dead rat in a field... in the night... in Washington state... having been killed... by whom... extreme that, or Writer, long walks, used garde body... mine with reserve, the Writer, wherein constructed, an empty hole where the employees smoked weed, the mine, they found stones nearby… though remembering… or extinct feedback… think, loop, the something, interested… ideal, psychedelic… in nothing, summer morning… confession, that—often accusing—quiet character… not, bent world… interested, already prog shoegazing out, writing, anxiety, worried… public interaction devices… music… pulsating noise… early Writer noise…

if there is in Writer—in this thing—Writer, don't… *in the thirtieth hour of the hijacking we each of us had to shit*… Writer has a form and a place in the universe and Writer guessed this meant something… *we had on thin leather jackets that were popular at the time*… Writer, look at the guitar… look at the instrument there… *we were gone from life and now we're someplace new, trapped*… Writer, guess, make a guess… in this in-between because what… Writer doesn't want to say liminal and Writer doesn't want to say interstitial… Writer believes a book can have a place within the world, especially wherein now the Goodwill store is now a place within the world… What happened to the media craze? What happened to the pursuit? What happened to our red and black thumbs and fingertips from sifting through the bootlegs? the fan… the Fan… Writer often forgets that Link Wray also sang… *we were criminals so what… we'd done something bad so what… you tell me you prove to me what we did was so much worse than some other thing*… Writer thinks people have lost the plot of living… by which Writer meant what… by which Writer meant Writer thinks people are very lost… his barometer for people being himself… *I'm a TV freak*… Writer doesn't care about jazz or the opera… Writer's a television addict… *here they come*… a part timer… the man sitting in his work clothes with a drink with the TV on… the part time punks… oh great… another person invested… another… another writer… the world needs another writer… Writer doesn't know if the world needs another anything… Writer doesn't know what the world needs… a pursuit… under some boot… another boot upon the neck and Writer's body is suspended there… if there is a writer in this thing it's Writer who is one of these morons you've been reading about… an emotional moron… no no, it isn't… it isn't him it's Writer in the apartment there in Washington there with his wife and daughter and his job at the gas station there… someone, moronic… Writer used to imagine walking into some city center and killing himself… things like that… *in the thirtieth hour of the hijacking everybody started shitting everywhere*… a sweaty American yelling… a sweaty foreigner sweating… someone somewhere doing something special, yes… the world is cumbersome… the world is around… everybody is there in the world screaming… regret sets in… you're sitting on the plane waiting to hear something and regret sets in… you're playing the gig and you're waiting to start a new song and regret sets in… the guitar on your neck is heavy… you look at the drummer… you look at the person manning the soundboard… you start to play a note and you start to sort of whisper into the microphone… it feels peaceful… you feel vulnerable… your hair is long… you're thin… you're very thin… you weigh almost nothing… you have a cavity in your chest… you start to sing… you start to sort of whisper hum… you're recording… you make sure he's recording… you try to make sure he's recording… everything is messy… everything has become messy… your girlfriend is mad at you… your records aren't selling… nobody's at the gig… nobody's…

here… nobody's here watching you… people want to talk to you about your choices… nobody is going to buy your record… nobody is going to buy your book… nobody is going to care… in two weeks your hijacking will be nothing… in two weeks your bootleg will be nothing… your instruments will be nothing… your ideas will be nothing… in two weeks… everything you've done will be nothing in two weeks… you have two more weeks to enjoy this and then you'll be dead… two weeks and soon you'll die… you can relax now… because soon you'll be dead… you can calm down now because you're going to die… one day this will all end… one day this suffering will stop… and it will be replaced by a new kind of suffering, a tenable suffering, a shaped suffering… no no… your life will end, and that is a relief… you're already dead… you're already dead… it should be a relief… you should be relieved about your death…

people tend to think of people who tell us highly liberative things that they lived in complete concurrence with these highly liberative things, consciously congruent with their idea… people don't want them, then, to be people… people want them to be the idea… people see them not as people, then… they grow in proximity to the popularity of their idea… they become figureheads… people like figureheads, people want a figurehead… Sartre himself was what… those teeth… Writer was drunk, sure… Writer was on drugs, in the forest, with the music playing… Writer was a hole in the ground… Writer was a person… Writer was a person in France, playing syringe chess with Alexander Trocchi… Writer was condemned to be free… to be free, to have that freedom… to be free meaning your life has only openings, potentials… you are stuck in these openings… your living is stuck in these contexts and these contexts are openings… or not, or, hm… his body, Writer or Trocchi… his eyes, a brick building you walk around to the back and see someone smoking and gesturing to join in… his eyes like yours, yellowy and bulbous… his lazy eyes like your lazy eyes… what was Writer drinking—coffee from a gas station in Washington… what was Writer doing, no no… what can any person do… how can any person make any pronouncement as a person within the world… how could any person sit there in the world… this body… this person in a body in the world… Writer cannot escape essence which is nothing… no, that isn't so… they are transcendent objects… that one European artist pissing in the mouth of that other European artist… *loud, fast, rules*… bodies there in the room there… what does any of it really amount too… being and nothingness… will and representation… people, and peopling… people in bathrooms… Enderby, meet me in the bathroom… you've finally got the mass market paperback of *Being and Nothingness* you've always wanted… Will you finally read it completely, then? possibly not… probably and possibly not… and that's OK… that's ok… that's O.K.… it's okay… you will sit on a bench on a train and you will sit in piss and realize you're in piss… Writer will see the woman with these sunken-in cheeks and Writer will not ask her anything and Writer will sit there and think through every possible situation which might transpire… on the street again alone Writer walks for ten miles and thinks and talks to himself and sneers and tries to figure out a way beyond the world… a man named Dan Buck comes into the gas station and gets a coffee and goes out into his car to sit drinking it and writing in a small notebook… Writer is condemned… shouts, moans, screamings… screams, metal, wood, skin… percussive noises… Writer is condemned to will and representation… his family goes to bed… he goes to see the film… he sits there and tries to experience it… he experiences it… Writer experiences the film… it feeds him something—a worm… Writer eats a worm and popcorn from the film… Writer goes home… Writer falls asleep on the couch in their apartment watching baseball…

Writer being in a course where a student presented on Anaïs Nin and thinking how stupidly the student was pronouncing her name, only to then realize that the student was pronouncing it correctly, and Writer was being an idiot… Writer thinks in many ways he's of this mindset regarding life… John Maus said one of his professors said that Maus was a musical thrills junkie… the idea of extremes appealed to him… the rest of it didn't… Writer thinks this is the case for him… no no… this means that reading a couple of pages of *Finnegans Wake* once a year makes more sense to Writer than simply sitting down and patiently reading *Ulysses*, even though the actual result might be more informative or engaging on a natural level… Writer read Freud saying there are two modes for someone to operate in, the analytic, or the synthetic… the synthetic mode was combinatory, but indicated immaturity… Writer was in the synthetic mode, not the analytic mode… no no… the fact that John Cage only really read *Finnegans Wake* when John Cage figured out a way of writing through it and incorporating it into his own process… in a lot of ways he's an idiot… Writer is dumb… Writer could have moments, though, where that dumbness throws itself into something more ambitious, and Writer guessed that was the long and short of himself and his work, or his desire for the work… Writer is not special… Writer is not different from any person… Writer doesn't write things off anymore… Writer differs from Nin here… *huh?* for a lot of his life Writer was that way… Writer wrote people off… Writer ran from things… Did Nin run? Writer…

deciding based on next to nothing that a person would be an obstacle on the way to whatever it was Writer was trying to conceive of and Writer wound up hurting and neglecting people because of this… Nin isn't describing being a sex addict… what is she describing… Nin is describing being a nymphomaniac… the difference is arguably negligible but only slightly… and in that slightness there is a practice and a life to be had… this, now, Writer guessed, is his life… it's made of fragments… Writer listened to them a bit the other day… a song came on shuffle… Writer hadn't thought about this work—this book—for weeks or longer… Writer had removed himself entirely from it, this… and now Writer returned… *one must be a god to tell successes from failures without making a mistake…*

this would explain the present moment's fascination with fractals, the fractal… Writer sits in the office drinking tea and trying to reach a level of peacefulness… Writer doesn't find a natural peacefulness… within Writer there isn't one… within Writer there's the anxious worm… *for indeed there is no goodness in the worm…* last night Writer's wife and Writer laughed over how disgusting Writer is… it wasn't melodramatic, he wasn't being melodramatic… Writer wasn't being a child, not then… Writer was… Writer *is*, legitimately disgusting in some ways… it's fine… it's OK… Writer guessed it was fine… Writer, sitting in the office now… coffee, coffee… Writer, afraid he'll be fired—*will it ever stop?* Writer's afraid he'll be stuck in this job forever... Writer is afraid... Writer watches John Fahey drunk sitting with a guitar... Writer thinks of someone's Telecaster... the shape of it... the extra materials on it... Writer thinks of his guitar... standing in a room... *we can't see the audience...* Writer likes that we can't see the audience... Writer's blood is boiling, or no... it's rising... no no... the orange seltzer water was perfect... tomorrow Writer will have an eye appointment... tomorrow Writer will have an eye appointment... no no... he'll get new glasses... no no... Writer is excited to get new glasses... no no... Writer doesn't know where he'll wind up... Writer is a mistake-maker... Writer makes mistakes... Julian Cope is nice... Pierre Menard is drunk... Mick Barr is nice... Mick Barr is Beethoven... Writer just received a rejection for this book... just now... Writer doesn't know how many rejections he's received in his life... Writer is a bit of a failure... Writer, a failure... Writer is an entire failure... Writer doesn't know what to do with his life besides write this... no no... this won't be published... no no... nobody will publish it... no no... nobody at all... nobody, anywhere... it won't be published...

Perhaps Writer didn't talk about it here... these things slip... forget Writer, for living, for even thinking about any of it, the Ōe way... Writer tried to be better than his father, and tried what... tried to be better than him in certain ways... Writer loved his father, and Writer what... Writer loved, and his father was a good man... a person who did his best in an unfair world, an ugly world… and Writer sees that now… no no… these days Writer finds it hard not to give up hope of amounting to something… no no… Writer hears things that don't exist… they act out… Writer knows that there is a sorrow outside in the world that Writer can't presently feel… a sorrow that would shock and reduce Writer to a stupid miserable state… no no… Writer hopes to what… Writer lives in a large apartment in his pajamas until Writer commits suicide… this is something depression will often communicate, sometimes screaming it at Writer… Writer wants to figure out how to live in a way that embraces the possibility that there is more to life than what's shoved down his throat at every turn… get real… it's depressing because of the lack of discrimination shown in pursuing that thing, but Writer understands it… understands what? it was a stupid phase in a series of a lot of stupid phases… *but I was different*… no no… the Flower Travellin' Band naked on their motorcycles… the fights… the immersion into the thing… romance of the black grief… people within the rooms… enter the mirror…

his modified guitar… his modified Telecaster guitar… Writer had heard about the stores in Japan… Writer had heard about these shops… everything being loud and being noxious… noisome… Writer doesn't know about the smoke… Writer remembers the hand being lifted up the audience member at the show and their movement around the world… things being played as loudly as they might… every picture the same guitar... no no... Writer thinks it's the same guitar... the thing being played is the same... maybe it's the same... his guest spot with that one group... the people who Writer played with too... Writer doesn't know if Writer would've talked to anybody there... Writer doesn't know who talked to whom... just a loud sound... a really loud sound over the crowd... people raising their hands up and screaming... people trying to sing something... a really loud sound... still they're riding motorcycles naked... the music being pummeling... Writer saw the loudest band he'd ever heard in the big former government building in Seattle... back in America, no no... Writer saw Prurient somewhere, some building... Pink Reason, that person, somewhere... Kevin, no no... Dominick Fernow, no no... playing where Writer was living... no no... this music hurting his stomach... having to leave... a heavyset man screaming... playing a simple recording of a man singing in another language... everything very loud... terribly loud... wearing leather jackets... black jackets... no no... wearing expensive black jackets... Writer had a bracelet from the show... no no... Writer found it on the ground... no no... Writer bought it when his father died... Writer bought a used partscaster and a small Orange amp that he's since sold... no no... Writer doesn't know why Writer sold them... Writer could've shown them to someone... the band... Writer could've been a part of them maybe, somehow... Writer doesn't know anymore... Writer could've joined them... no no... Writer could've had a place somewhere in there… no no… Writer, his wasted life… no no… Writer has a body and Writer has wasted his life… his living… Writer has wasted his living flesh… he'll be a corpse soon enough… he'll get a new guitar… he'll get something new and he'll sing a song… he'll do something new… he'll name it after the bunny Daisy… someday… his father never died…

although Writer suspects that people do tend to over-emphasize this notion of being awake, of being freed, or being somehow shaken loose from this state wherein we no longer live under the iron boot of whatever, Writer still finds truth in the sentiments… it's a miracle that Nin existed, that she wrote, that she wrote what she did and it was shared, that it's available, that it's a thing that exists in the world, that it's even a thing that Writer can check out from most any library, it's a miracle… it's a miracle that any person has ever done anything, sure… but Nin transcends most human things, transcends Miller certainly, transcends honesty and Pepys, sure, perhaps even Robert Shields, though let's not go there, not yet… or manages, or people manage, or how do the people manage… Writer doesn't know how someone does something… for instance, where do you start? And do you record it? Writer used to walk off into the woods in Washington, no no, where Writer was born and Writer would imagine Seymour Glass and Writer would imagine getting a cabin for himself and going there to write something and filming himself and somehow entering this multimedia spectacle thing of the process and Writer guessed it had to do with Seymour Glass and this sense that that is what Writer might've done and Writer thought about this a lot…

every time he'd walk, until one day Writer went home, and Writer doesn't know if he was married, and if his daughter was born, their first daughter, and it might've been early morning—it was—and nobody was awake… and Writer had gone out walking into the same country, and Writer thinks he brought some music with him, and Writer kept walking, and Writer never thought of Seymour Glass, and all Writer had failed to do to live up to that… What do you do if your entire output has been a bootleg? Has been in the form of a bootleg? Has been this thing that wasn't put together by you? sometimes it feels like that… you'd like for it to feel like that… it would be convenient if it felt like that… but it can't, it doesn't, and really it's like the earlier, worse, dumber version of yourself just had too much freedom… and if you could've gone back and strangled that self and given him something to say then maybe… there's no music, there isn't a sound to make… a man walks onto the stage and he has a brown SG and the sound that he manages to extract from it is incredible… over and over and over again these sounds being repeated and layered on top of one another and there are no pedals to speak of… nothing to enhance the experience but him, this instrument, and this cord, and this amplifier, and that's it… and two hundred copies of your book printed that's enough… and two hundred copies of your record pressed that's enough... and two hundred dollars in your bank account that's enough... and a Squier to figure your shit out that's enough... maybe someday something old... the Teisco the partscaster... and these books these music books are that... they are cobbled together... they are surfiction... they are critifiction... sure, sure... why not... they are whatever you say they are... the Partscaster Trilogy... the Nocilla Generation... a TV show of someone playing a recording of someone sitting in a room and doing something insane, something criminal... *let's go do some crimes... let's go out and do some crimes*... great... another white suburban punk... another car... another tan Toyota Tacoma with a camper bed... the same color as the can of your Vanilla Coke Zero... a cup of coffee... a can of Celsius... photograph all the perfume in the house... what is with the perfume fascination... a bottle of *Angel* which apparently smells like excrement... a bottle of *Aromatics Elixir* which apparently makes you hallucinate... a small simple bottle almost shaped like a little purple apple from the time of World War II available on eBay for seven hundred dollars... buy it, purchase it... sit in your room with it and see what you feel... and does it smell the same... and is there some sort of fermentation process... and what is that process... and how is perfume like literature... and how are smells like sentences... and how are sounds like sentences... and what does the guitar smell like, after all this time... it smells like cement in the rain... and what did that plane smell like... it smelled like shit… like *Angel*… and what did the venue smell like… it smelled like wet cement and bodies, dirt… and in the morning, when the gig was done, and everybody was finished, did they walk up out of the basement…

leathers… and did steam express from their shoulders and wetted hair, and was snow falling like in that film, simply, like the old man sitting on the swing, Toshiro Mifune, or someone else, and as the snow fell did one of them, the American among them, Writer among them, the one contracted to write about the scene for who, for Lester Bangs' ghost, or Richard Meltzer, or someone else, did Writer have pieces of Orange Sunshine, and did Writer hand it to them, and did they put it on their tongues in the forest, beneath the great green arbors, and did the bandmembers join them, and did they smoke, and as it dissolved on their tongues was the noise still ringing in their ears, and did they walk upstairs after staring at the sun as the chemical began to wend its way through their guts and blood, and were they awakened in that moment, and were they pure, and did one of them strum his twelve-string guitar as they lay on the ground, smoke rising from their mouths, the sun rising there on the opposing side of the city, nobody writing and nobody painting, nobody recording and nobody performing, nobody speaking and nobody weeping, a pot of tea then in the center of the room and each one of them somehow touching the limb of each other one next to them, a circle of flesh…

Writer, don't, do not… think, anxiety, anxious… life, a long dumb time… things, dumb… people are around and they're commenting on living on the internet and it's untenable and things are warping again and commingling again and nothing is making sense… in the world nothing is making sense to Writer… Writer wrote a book about a cow… a simple cow… a moocow on the ground or the road… a moocow sleeping on the ground or the road, however the moocow slept… Writer wrote the book… Writer didn't market the book to children… Writer didn't market the book… Writer might've marketed the book to children because it was a childlike book… Writer didn't write the book for children, though… or… Writer could be stupid that way… sure… Writer would do stupid things, sure… Writer would rent a hotel room just to sit on the floor of the shower in his clothes through several cycles of the water cooling and heating up again… Writer wrote… no no… Writer ate a sandwich… no no… Writer read a piece of paper… Writer applied for a new job… Writer watched a TV show about a cow named Robert… Writer watched Robert Mitchum… Writer wrote Robert Mitchum a letter… Writer wrote a letter to a cow… a cow named Robert Mitchum… sure, OK… Writer adopted an animal… Writer helped the chickens… Writer took an ugly shower… Writer kissed the bunny on the head… Writer was eaten by a tractor… Writer had a room in a hotel and gave it to a cow…

We cannot live outside our bodies, our friends, some sort of human cluster, and at the same time, we are bursting out of this situation. The question which poses itself then is one of the conditions which allow the acceptance of the other, the acceptance of a subjective pluralism. It is a matter not only of tolerating another group, another ethnicity, another sex, but also of a desire for dissensus, otherness, difference. Accepting otherness is a question not so much of right as of desire. This acceptance is possible precisely on the condition of assuming the multiplicity within oneself. (Guattari)

of the world in which Writer lived... Writer, too, pretty much done with writing, not being a writer anymore... maybe never having been a writer, Writer... Writer precisely on the condition of assuming the multiplicity within oneself... not oneself... Writer's self... the multiplicity within Writer's one self... sure... Writer didn't take care of himself... Writer didn't... life being this thing Writer was bad at... Writer, not having any talent for it... living... nor did Writer take care of the condition of assuming the multiplicity within oneself... it's this anxiety shared, Writer wished it were not... multiplicity, or... it's time... in pain, heaven... and otherwise to believe, starting around Writer—that writer—exactly... no no... maybe Writer should try, says Editor, and thinks to quit writing, Writer... no no... overcoat, and nothing... who... Writer loving regretting... kind, nightmares with blood... Writer, free... see to its flaws... Writer encourages a world of points... of confession... or they're too personal sort of, they'd shot anything remotely regretting living... OK... Writer, the extreme fleeting sense of the work... sufferings for, or limited in—when—lots, for a time... and writers, and none function quite... no no... none of them quite function... about which, one of them, as a ghost, is older... sees a crack, arm in arm... walk on... the book, and Writer both... were love's purveyors... in its leaves that day... we read no more...

Writer can't escape the notion that he's probably a poser and this informs every moment in his life... a dilettante... someone for whom the things which seem accessible for others aren't exactly accessible... when he's walking it's different... no it isn't... when he's able to go out and go for a walk it changes... L.R.D.'s music... something changes... Writer can listen to music and feel as though it's hitting him at a particular level... L.R.D.'s music... the music of the group... their music from a soundboard or possibly it's not even them... the nature of the bootleg... this exhilarated him... Chris Ott holding different bootleg editions of Aphex Twin... who? nobody... a screen somewhere... making these sounds... driving in the wet sun to get coffee... Writer can think about things and believe in things... no no... Albert Ayler can... Peter Brötzmann can... no no... residing Thelema... L.R.D. can... Writer can believe in something, in abilities... no no... in voices... no no... and then he's standing in a field, outside of a church... in the middle of nowhere in Washington, surrounded by adult men and women, and Writer walks around nervously acting as though he's pursuing the ball, like Writer wants to participate, but really he's just killing time until the game ends... until the world ends... until his life ends... no no... Writer had to accept that Writer wasn't cool, could be a poser... good... Writer, arcade, socialist... Writer had to accept that Writer couldn't be a cool person... Writer couldn't look cool... Writer couldn't come across as cool, and maybe this was fine, and maybe the idea of being cool was a little stupid... Writer sweated profusely... through all of his layered shirts... through his vests... Writer sat at work at the gas station sweating, and trying to focus, and people coming and going... sweating through shirts, Writer... when Writer was a boy Writer would have days where somehow he'd convince his mother to go to the store where they sold rollerblades... and he'd buy them, and he'd bring them home and he'd fetishize them, and that was something... no no... he'd look at guitars online, now, as an adult, and imagine owning every one Writer wanted... no no... this was something... this wasn't nothing... this wasn't something cool... Writer wasn't going to be cool... Writer wasn't going to share a video of himself playing an Electrical Guitar Company guitar and have two thousand people look at it and be cool in this very unassuming way... *no*... Writer wasn't going to do that, couldn't do that... his daughter was trying to learn something... Writer liked taking her to piano... Writer had to help her learn something and Writer had to realize

Writer didn't know how to read music, and Writer felt small, and very pathetic, and the feeling stayed with him as Writer went about the rest of his day...

Writer would talk about things, talk about guitars or books or music or films, and Writer would feel as though Writer was wasting whoever's time, and that feeling wouldn't leave him, and Writer wasn't sure what to make of it, and the world seemed fine with him feeling this way, and the world offered no way forward... Writer remembered the box... the library where Writer got his degree in Washington... Writer suddenly realized Writer could check out so many different things, and there was no limitation put on them, and Writer remembered when older the box he'd gotten from there containing tons of books and films, and Writer remembered carrying them to his car, as he'd once carried a dead bird to his car, and Writer realized Writer still did it today, and Writer got these things, and Writer didn't read them, and Writer bought books, and Writer rented books, and Writer bought films, and Writer bought albums, and Writer liked albums on Bandcamp, and Writer never listened, and Writer never found a way to get back to some sense that there was merit in any of it, and Writer felt this fraudulence, and Writer looked around to see the world in its confidence, but didn't walk, getting fatter...

Have to be accountable. Yield to arguments. What I feel like is just fucking around. Publish this diary for example. Say stupid shit. Barf out the fucking-around-

*o-maniacal schizo flow. Barter whatever for whoever wants to read it. Now that I'm turning into a salable name I can find an editor for sure [...] Work the **feedback**; write right into the real.* (Guattari)

Writer has said this before... Writer is sure of it... nobody is communicating... nobody is saying anything... they're performing... live at the gallery... three of them... be sure you're not repeating yourself... the Ōe way... you're getting old... you're getting older now... the last one_1970... your body is getting older old man... Writer is living on the ground and moaning like a dog... the dead dog... their dead dog who used to sit with him at the piano... Writer sitting at the piano... Writer making sounds... no no... a body in a room and people screaming around them... the guitar isn't the thing... no no... the performance isn't the thing... no no... the word isn't the thing... the TV is a hole... the body isn't the thing... nobody is around... their fascist aesthetics... define fascism... no no... nobody talking... a podcast... a person... a woman... two women... a room... two bodies... a room... nobody speaking... the guitar making sounds... dressed in that way... in a leather jumpsuit... with the instrument... we need an instrument... America's just a word... no no... nobody talk... nobody make a sound... Writer not making a sound... Writer in the city... Writer on the ground in the city... Writer smoking crack... somebody offering Writer crack... a small doorway... nobody's there... a man is standing there... no no... *I can see him there*... offering you crack... no no... everybody becoming quieted... the sound becoming dull... no no... everybody speaking... the world living... people being alive and not stopping... people everywhere living... Writer living... everybody talking... the people on the internet talking... speaking... somebody saying something... somebody being elected... a room in Washington... a room in Oregon...

walking along the beach... Writer took a starfish... stolen... the starfish had a barnacle attached to it... it looked disgusting... soaked in bleach... it dies... a new kind of guilt... a pure kind... a purity... it isn't nice... nothing about it feels OK... everything feels terrible as the band plays... too much speed... too much... too much adrenaline... too much coffee... dehydrated... no water... go somewhere and sit down... the skinhead says something... he's talking to you... he wanted to talk to you... you always wanted to talk to him... he was cool... Writer fucked up... Writer wrote him... the band is changing... the footage changes... he's so skinny... he's so skinny... his body there... his body in the room... you're repeating yourself again... it's been one big repetition... it's never going to stop... you don't need drums... if it's loud enough you won't need them... buy a guitar... tune it way down... Keiji Haino's bangs... everybody talking... their robes... the band talking... people living... people in America living... in Paris... in Japan... a guitar being played slowly... a woman's voice, singing... everybody quieting down... it's simple... like James'

song… it's stupid… it's pop… it feels emotional…
it makes you scared like when you were young…
scared of what it made you feel… scared to be that
young…

*Obsessives try in vain and without respite to interrupt
the progress of deterritorialization. They want to hold
on, once and for all, to **the** real sequence, **the** best
interpretation. They fight against history, time, death.
If they talk about them so much, it's to conjure them up.
The stakes of their fanatical perfectionism are pathetic.
What matters is not the nature of realization, but the
extinction of a burning break: the incessant search,
never to hear anything else again, for a sort of drug that
would make all other threatening voice(s) of desiring
machinism shut up.* (Guattari)

Joe Wenderoth says a poem should be like a beef
bouillon cube… no no… for Writer, it's more like
he'll see someone wearing something and feel as
though it's indicative of their personality, or their
state within the world… and Writer will envy them
for that apparent state and Writer will buy something
similar, maybe… Writer practices a sort of frantic
walking… but even then Writer feels like a fool for
trying to theorize his way back to walking… Writer
sees things or animals or people around him that
others do not see… Writer is trying… get a lawyer…
Writer had the first seizure, and was in one room,
and had no girlfriend… no no… you're repeating
yourself… Writer worries about how Writer comes
across… many people treat Writer more like a child

than a grown-up… no no… this isn't because Writer doesn't respect people but because Writer does… Writer likes Boosie… no no… fuck Karl Ove… Writer sometimes teases animals… Writer doesn't know that Writer is independent either, but he's trying to embrace the things he likes and not feel such shame about being a pretty average person… Writer doesn't want for anybody to have a job… no no… Writer can't do that… Writer is working on it… evil spirits possess Writer at times… pure evil… Writer is a writer, and a miserable, inward-facing person who's trying hopelessly to figure something out… no no… sometimes when Writer was young Writer stole things… no no… Did Writer already write about that in this book? Writer thinks Writer might've… no no…

iii.   Do we stray
into infinite
nothingness? (F.N.)

it's stupid, in living—in living this way, living, one cannot say… life is something else… Writer, with, no—no no—every every day… people, sort of, peopling… an academic, and what of the academic… no no… an attendant, and where, in the gas station… to wonder whether capable of *being* sadness… no no… Writer was coffee then, in the morning… as written Writer was drawn closer, closer, sure… people are a trouble, are troubling—peopling… everything, that's all of his thinking… in, in what— between thoughts—which iteration—Writer, too forced—Writer, to this… if such a living—what— tedious Writer, of opportunity anymore… no no… and as Writer, basis is a soul… it sleepwalks every single day… always, *The Sleepwalkers*… Writer, though wanting and asking—somehow fucking it up, fucking even that up too… using animal, and human voices… stone, baked earth, etc.… fuck you, Writer… want, things—fuck you, too… Writer's anxiety, given meds to do the opposite, of what—Writer is a twitching tunnel… when Writer jolts, othered, and everybody around Writer, feeling just, in continuing… Writer—we'd seen not—in that building, or—and disoriented—gets tired sometimes, when Writer still believed that—bored, asked Editor to read—much the terrible thing… into Writer's situation Editor doesn't know what Writer would, or why… it is soon…

Only look about you: blood is being spilt in streams, and in the merriest way, as though it were champagne. Take the whole of the nineteenth century in which Buckle lived. Take Napoleon—the Great and also the present one. Take North America—the eternal union. Take the farce of Schleswig-Holstein .... And what is it that civilisation softens in us? The only gain of civilisation for mankind is the greater capacity for variety of sensations—and absolutely nothing more. And through the development of this many-sidedness man may come to finding enjoyment in bloodshed. In fact, this has already happened to him. Have you noticed that it is the most civilised gentlemen who have been the subtlest slaughterers, to whom the Attilas and Stenka Razins could not hold a candle, and if they are not so conspicuous as the Attilas and Stenka Razins it is simply because they are so often met with, are so ordinary and have become so familiar to us. In any case civilisation has made mankind if not more bloodthirsty, at least more vilely, more loathsomely bloodthirsty. In old days he saw justice in bloodshed and with his conscience at peace exterminated those he thought proper. Now we do think bloodshed abominable and yet we engage in this abomination, and with more energy than ever. (F.D.)

or, Writer—have—about new swollen appendices, the diary—the ideal form, perhaps the only form, the only ideal, the only honest text... and Robert Shields the purest practitioner, or one of them... perhaps Sade and perhaps Pepys... no no... do something... *wrong*, wrong... hands and people and working and debt... only debt... fish there, fish to... no no... or fish out there, without, within the world, being, and living... try to at least appear... being, *being*... projects left one feeling hobbled, a form both of us... or no, and Writer, up on... upon, Writer, it... inward, to well over—was—have relief... that someone, that somehow someone's too sure... was in the life thus... different, stumble... Writer—don't... Writer—gossip... Writer—deading... deadheading flowers, room... Writer of—no no... to them, and that life, depressive we... the depressive we, Writer, a me, no no... everything made poison, the thought being poison... Writer, writer, Writer writer writer writer Writer writer... sentence, Writer... understand it... no no... *the New Testament Writer who uses the word antichrist is the so-called Apostle John; and it is interesting to remark that it is by him connected with a dogmatic statement of the nature of Christ and definition of heresy...* 'Every spirit that confesses Jesus Christ is come in the flesh is of God; and every spirit that confesses not Jesus is not of God: and this is the spirit of antichrist, whereof ye have heard that it comes; and now it is in the world already... Writer once read a description of the difference between representing someone in ordinary legal matters and in legal matters of this sort, and they expressed it very well... this is what they said: some lawyers lead their clients on a thread until judgement is passed, but there are others who immediately lift their clients onto their shoulders and carry them all the way to the judgement and beyond... that's just how it is... visions... a writer—Writer, nothing... a, like, and... don't fly there people... how really Minnesota, very middle...

slowly repeating every single thing... Writer going to work in the morning and putting on the gray pants and the white shirt and the shoes from Walmart and driving... walking into work... nobody listening... people stopping by... his wife texts him... everything is stressful... the world is full of stress... falling apart... they're in debt... they're broke and in debt... they're stuck... Writer on acid back in Japan falling asleep on the snowy ground outside of the home after tea with each of them... they're next to him and they're not going to leave... they're Writer's friends... they're going to spend the day together... they're going to spend every day together... the social animal... their clothing... the denim... the leather... the metal... their hair... their eyes... their tired eyes... Writer's eyes on the ground... on the sun... the sun...

rising... the hidden fortress... today they take more acid and drink more tea... they go into the forest... they find the fortress... they find George Lucas... they find the fortress... they're young... army jackets and leather jackets... smelly, young, angry, sleeping... their bodies sleeping... nothing to say... watching TV... listening to records... listening to whining... listening to Americans... they grab an instrument... nobody grabs an instrument... no no... someone sits at the drums... they're seeing a show... Peter Brötzmann playing live with someone... in a club... in a club in the city in Japan... no no... he screams... they watch it and they scream... Writer screams... Writer listens and screams… Writer listens to music… Writer listens to the music… Writer takes the music into his body… it is L.R.D.'s music… it is something… it is the sound of the music… the resonance, the feedback… the form… everything falling apart…

If this diary is ever published—and it's written like it should be—then I am setting myself up for all kinds of strange encounters! Well, so be it! An analyst, more than anyone else, has to be held accountable, and supply, publicly, for example every year, an updated report on his little company. Enough two-faced office practice secrets, with a "pious" respect for privacy… short-circuit the singular and the universal: what doesn't stand the test of light has to die. (Guattari)

and a sadness, an everlasting dull ache… Writer would work—the addiction becomes the work… Writer wondered what he was doing… being a person… the book, in it, personally… about what… loyalty, sure… improve on that, Writer, not Writer… Writer, like to a clinical perspective, Writer can't be efficient, can Writer… whatever else… Writer worries… Writer's then-life… Writer's ego taking a beating… Writer being very depressed… Writer feeling like there's nothing, there was nothing good to Writer… Writer feeling pathetic… Writer apologizing constantly… Writer being consumed with guilt… Writer's medicine not working… minutes, and a TV's music to tap by word out on—at—Writer's balcony… or who… in retrospect the fictional can't work like an intrusive thought—

Writer no longer making any distinction at all... Writer this—not, no—yours... an ambulance and wish that Writer becomes them... a crack-up... Writer's crack-up... crackup... the whole thing... the whole ball of wax... adaptive to light... Writer worries, new sitting, small work...

romanticism, symbolism... pataphysics, dadaism... form, conjunctive, closed... antiform, disjunctive, open... purpose, play, design, chance, hierarchy, anarchy, no no... mastery, logos... exhaustion, silence... art object, finished work... process, performance, happening... distance, participation... creation, totalization... decreation, deconstruction... synthesis, antithesis... presence, absence... centering, dispersal... genre, boundary, text, intertext... semantics, rhetoric... paradigm, syntagm... hypotaxis, parataxis... metaphor, metonymy... selection, combination... root, depth... rhizome, surface... interpretation, reading... against interpretation, misreading... signified, signifier... lisible, readerly... scriptable, writerly... narrative, grande histoire... anti-narrative, petite histoire... master code, idiolect... symptom, desire, type, mutant... genital, phallic... polymorphous, androgynous... paranoia, schizophrenia... origin, cause... difference-differance, trace... God the father, the holy ghost... metaphysics, irony... determinacy, indeterminacy... transcendence, immanence... yet the dichotomies this table represents remain insecure, equivocal. For differences shift, deter, even collapse; concepts in any one vertical column are not all equivalent; and inversions and exceptions, in both modernism and postmodernism, about. (Hassan)

Writer what, Writer searches for a picture, pictures of someone in some film—not him—and someone else, someone older, not the Writer, while watching something else… the internet was full of nepotism and New York City was a hole in which to take a curmudgeonly shit… a magazine was being published, people were fucking each other or taking drugs… a play was being performed in which the performers backed into a circle and took a shit collectively so their efforts commingled… no no… Writer is sympathetic about guitars, or not guitars, or not sympathetic—the things made him feel a wholeness, a completeness—or too worshipful… too caught up… money was everywhere… the money, money everywhere and none of it Writer's, Writer can look at guitars for a long time… anywhere, in any context… he, Writer, likes to look at guitars and to consider buying them, if he had money, if he had the money, if only… Writer wants to buy all he can, an endless life of buying whatever… Writer doesn't want to buy all he can, or no… and now the pens, becoming obsessed with buying pens, OHTO pens… looking back, from which dumb American reason is… no no… a half-hollow lawsuit guitar, gutted, the author played it without any amplifier… someone had performed surgery on it… no no… his friend stopped by and Writer brought him collected things, fetishized things… no no… in most areas of his life Writer, who… no no… the item, something to make him whole… book, Bookworm with Michael Silverblatt, a boot… forager, operator, money, chest of drawers… Writer came up with a list of gear and whatever to wear in the snow once on vacation in Mexico, the whole flight going both ways to look around and think about his life...

all these different ways, no... the shoes, no no... Writer's parents talked about Imelda Marcos... Writer didn't look her up or see her picture, no no... she had lots of shoes... Writing of shoes is good, no no... to write of that devotion... the Menthol 10 sneaker, Writer's dream... Writer liked rollerblades... no no... Writer liked the winter, snow clothing... no no... in between, in living, in living this way and fixating on objects... Writer liked watching videos... Writer didn't like it so much, living... no no... have a bad day, you—*thank you*... the Writer, now and then, he might from a friend's home, sure... sad, yeah, sad... he watches a video with his mom nearby and he talk about wanting something, new sneakers or something worse... sometimes he gets a new pair or a spare or something... no, in 1998, this was in 1998, no no, this was in 1999... in America it was so strong that no one really thought about it and for years it dies, it died—past tense—it was dead... writing, in living, living Writer wrote in dying ever dying... when it happened, like everything, he went to his friend's house or went down into a hole in the hillside and wept there... these hill towns in Washington, there are a lot of dirty places to put together a wooden plank and try something... it seems to work... he's going up but still afraid of, of more, of going anywhere, of hiding this way or going out... and he watches videos, more videos...

he watches the hand, so the movies show it… he makes friends and they bring drugs or weapons or cans of paint into the hillside… he looks at his hand, his own hand there… watches some video and then takes them off, or takes off, maybe he doesn't… he watches a video of Larry Clark on the street in Paris… there is a department, from his dad's stuff, from his store… *they are coming back and coming like inside…* wearing clothes, a big t-shirt and sweatpants… a poser, a… it is like that… maybe they're going to a party renting movies or video games… *it's 1998… you have a Nintendo 64 with a gold screen… you order a pizza with extra cheese… your friends arrive… four of them…* grumpy bags… *you don't know now but it's a good life…* (Flores) his friends have what the Writer didn't know he needed when he was working… the Writer is lazy, will laze… Writer is lazy… Writer is prodigiously lazy… nothing wrong, what… Writer talks, will talk… Writer spins through magazines, TV channels… just laughing, O shut the hell up, just laugh… Writer compares himself to people… constantly, it doesn't stop… they do, the people do, they walk and they live and they're everywhere… the next days he's alone in his room… see someone, a girl, chase girls… listening to music, alone… hanging out in the river… gas station bathroom… looking for drugs… one night some friends and Writer hid in an abandoned barn drinking cough syrup late into the night… they drink, whatever—later… he was at their house at night and they smoked something, he was confused… he was eleven then… it seems like ten years but it's clear, a hole… it's not, it turns,

turns, turns... someone puts on an L.R.D. tape, taking, taking... music now, now great music... now fooling around jumping from heights in the barn... now stealing, still, still... still struggling, a hole... it's time for the forest to stop... watch my steps to follow, see... the sides are given... *not obstructed by flames, all fog has lifted from them...*

There is no such thing as a father in general. There is only a father who works at the bank, who works in a factory, who is unemployed, who is an alcoholic: the father is only the element of a particular social machine. According to traditional psychoanalysis, it's always the same father and always the same mother— always the same triangle. But who can deny that the Oedipal situation differs greatly, depending on whether the father is an Algerian revolutionary or a well-to-do executive? It isn't the same death which awaits your father in an African shanty town as in a German industrial town; it isn't the same Oedipus complex or the same homosexuality. It may seem stupid to have to make such statements, and yet such swindles must be denounced tirelessly: there is no universal structure of the human mind! (Guattari)

DOMESTIC PUNK,
IT WAS EVENING,
NIGHT WAS
BEGINNING TO
SPREAD,
THE BLACKNESS
OF HER VEIL OVER
NATURE—I AM
FILTHY, I AM
RIDDLED WITH
LICE—HOGS,
WHEN THEY LOOK
AT ME, VOMIT

Minnesota Multiphasic Personality Inventory

Man is an oak. There is no more robust in nature. There is no need for the whole universe to take arms to defend him. A drop of water is not enough for his preservation. (Ducasse)

when Writer takes a new job, Writer likes to find out whom it is important to be nice to… Writer had these sweats in the early morning because overnight Writer dreamt of the forest, or Pascal… Writer sweated and Writer sweated and Writer stood in front of people and Writer stands there looking pathetic in his new job and miserable and Writer talks and if he's had coffee then Writer sweats more but Writer talks more and so it's easier… no no… Writer doesn't like to watch the new films… no no… Writer is within an anxiety, an anxious state, a hole… this is correct for Writer, although his wife often suffers more from this and Writer worries about her… Writer is interested in anything that forces a person into a position of extremity… his relatives are nearly all in sympathy with him… Writer would get something to eat, or should… no no… this is tough, as he's not sure what they mean by "health," and he's not sure what they mean by "friends"… David Bowie explored the fascists, in turn, or no… David Bowie did piles of cocaine and called Adolf Hitler one of the first rockstars… Writer is interested in anything that forces a person into a position of extremity… when people do him wrong, Writer feels he should pay them for it, just for doing him wrong and hopefully ruining things… it's definitely tied with Writer's present desire to quit writing, not because

Writer doesn't love writing, but because Writer feels as though Writer persists in trying, and persists in keeping pushing on, only to find himself in exactly the same place every moment of his living… it's as if you're there, and you're feeling that the presence of potential death is so loud, that you feel as though you should jump just to complete this apparently logical action in such an absurd circumstance… not only does Writer do this once in a while, but most of the time, if not all of the time… no no… it's stupid, so stupid…

apparently constant reassurance, intimacy, home-based hobbies, are things which would appeal to or be natural things to Writer—these seem useful, probably, as a person has to kind of situate themselves within the world, and that's kind of stupid, a person should be able to just be a person, but they can't just be people—Writer can't just be a person, no no—because of the ways in which the world works, and stupid things like circumstance, or whatever… it makes a person become forced to do things which might refute their nature, or something, and then a person is fucked, as all people are fucked, and thus we tell ourselves stuff as Writer tells himself stuff… to not be such a gigantic piece of shit and waste of shit… and a show to watch… and mayonnaise… and nonsense is a kind of sense, a version of it… and people are moving around… and the end was the perfect iteration… and that's rare… and you listened to it happening… Writer listened to "My Girl is a Boy" by Your Old Droog… Writer listened to *And*

Who Shall Go to the Ball? And Who Shall Go to the Ball?... Writer listened to "People Can Choose" by L.R.D., or "Ice Fire"... or *Balls...* or *Bells...* or *Nuits de la Fondation Maeght Vol. 1...* or *Spiritual Unity...* and in it found the word of something whole... and in it found the word of something whole... and in the glitchy changing things were going on... a phone upon the bed the TV going at night... a dog asleep, is sleeping... a dog on the TV... Albert Ayler meet Peter Brötzmann... meet L.R.D.... meet the Nobody... meet the Nobody walking around the room with their shirt off... the Nobody of avant jazz... the Editor, the Writer... go to bed...

a little fond of loathsome historical aberrations... no no... no thing holds Writer quicker than a wonderful cop... no no... got the floor now pay attention... no no... Writer listened for years to the people who sing... dead idiots... the instrument being played with the mouth—the glass—is a kind of singing... *Justice Yeldham, my only friend...* a bit of a corpse, you see it yes, you can see it, yes? put this word here and then include a word which would end the sentence... ending the sentences for you, for Writer... put this word here and then include a word which would end the sentence... end this sentence just as soon as Writer started it... good-looking men and women shopping for saws... my son is named No and he's an avid fan of Howard Hughes, or strawberry milk... yes of course Howard Hughes the madman but had it been strawberry milk, what then? *welcome to the park—gotta steal your car... the light from that slipper is blinding me...* listen up, dipshit, going to steal your brand new car... good boy, Writer says to the fish—picked up... no no... behold with what—companions—Writer walked the streets of Babylon and wallowed in the mire thereof, as if in a bed of spices and precious ointments... noxious plume of your dogshit personage happened upon by an evening walking spy... Writer can see the cows upon the hill from where Writer sits in Walmart's lot... the evening walking spy... the red car breathes a snotty smell... the blue car dipped its nose into the small mound of shit upon the ground... Writer mixed two doubled cups of tea within the large Nalgene bottle with its Yeti sticker... no no... Writer bought a shirt and two books... the smell of piss adorns my every cloth... Writer has on his Adidas hat... good weepy eyes upon the lover's gnarling dimple... no no... one side of their face is subdued, a palsy, like Conway the Machine... no no... Writer saw upon the slew a bit of rock Writer longed to tongue... Writer filled his cheeks with salty rocks from along the ocean's side... whom, womb, restlessness... Writer has no teeth and so the rocks were comforts, with which to gum... every gnawing made him better in his standing... his living thus enhanced, Writer went in for a swim... the short was gray like the water... the air was gray like the sand... his body went out into the waters there in dim light... the cold water from the ocean poured in... his anxiety went out of him like the moors... his body white in the dark water and the wet death… his body didn't stop its churning within the icy waves until he'd shat and slowly ambled back to find his clothing…

Writer then upon the ground… Writer went for soup within the village and heard an old man playing his guitar… no no… Writer does not think… Writer had his bicycle… every morning Writer wakes up and buries his face in a mound of mold he's kept in the corner of his bathroom… it's black, and stinking… outside, the rocks in his teeth, they're black… all black, his mouth a stinking hole… Writer inhales deeply through his nose and mouth then urinates out the window onto his neighbor's deck… no no… his piss is redolent with death… no no… Writer sees the bodies of runners slowly fucking their ways up the stupid streets… no no… Writer goes into the local thing… whatever, whatever… Writer buys a local piece of shit… Writer takes it outside into the lot and crawls under the van… Writer opens up the oil and lets it empty onto his stinking body, his stinking skin… laughter, rattlings, sobs… Writer walks down the street while it goes away… no no… people are always behaving like such gigantic piles of filth… no no… how high can the blood boil up… sure, sure… how much more of your spit can Writer borrow… cut the lingual shit with your magnificent caterwauling you insufferable cop… no no… cut it, quiet it, address the reader… mere pseud mag ed… sorry, sorry… another quiet morning atop the sea of shit within the bustling world of the Americans… yea, yeah…

hello, Phil, good morning… welcome home Phil you're home here… good day, rest up… eat a filet upon the buffet… *I can't do that, Dave…*

He left the stage quickly and rid himself of his mummery and passed out through the chapel into the college garden. Now that the play was over his nerves cried for some further adventure. He hurried onwards as if to overtake it. The doors of the theatre were all open and the audience had emptied out. On the lines which he had fancied the moorings of an ark a few lanterns swung in the night breeze, flickering cheerlessly. He mounted the steps from the garden in haste, eager that some prey should not elude him, and forced his way through the crowd in the hall and past the two jesuits who stood watching the exodus and bowing and shaking hands with the visitors. He pushed onward nervously, feigning a still greater haste and faintly conscious of the smiles and stares and nudges which his powdered head left in its wake. (Joyce)

quiet down… long has Writer wished to plug his fist through his own wiry socket and see what pops out… no no… a glutton for big meandering idiots…no no… so grateful to see you all father it… so grateful to see you all gathered here in Dallas… for someone somewhere it was the greatest day of their life… for someone it was the end of a long path, a simple conclusion on top of a big fat cake… mine eyes have big dusty polyps when Writer goes to the top of their ladders and prepares himself to die… so grateful to the city of Phoenix… *I'm so glad*

I'm dead now… what a wonderful weeping morning on Washington—in Washington… upon the Washington… upon the river… Pete Seeger upon the river going there… his body there, the old man… welcome to the bubbling river, idiot… welcome to all idiots upon the river… it's the day on which the bodies will be buoys in their tubes… Writer likes to go beneath them to look at the diseases they leak upon the oils… *make me some popcorn you illiterate fuckhead!* now now, we won't have any of that now now… moocow nope not now… good dog upon the now now… good whispering dipshit dog illiterate upon the now now… Writer not now… Writer, embody a husk upon the ground with the corn… shuck me and cut my head off, my living head… good idea you insufferable idiot… good welcome idea on the morning of you, your—idiot… Writer can't, Writer can't wait to see you get married to the police… Writer just can't wait any longer… Writer wanted you to understand… Writer reached back into the guts of time and tried to pull an apple out… why would anyone deny Eve her apple… you're a piece of shit if you want a person not to eat an apple… unless they're your allergic child… *O shut the fuck up you sentimental bore*… kiss a stump upon the shit if you—if you—if—dumb ground and feed your head through a sleeve of lambskin… great, great… another dumb idea from a dumb asshole… a wonderful time to be alive and to witness yourself becoming a corpse… Writer will leave a heaving corpse… Writer will leave behind him a NASCAR driver corpse…

Writer will get one of those jackets... like Dave Hickey, Dave Hickey's jacket... Writer will get one of those jackets... Writer will smoke cigarettes in Las Vegas, like Dave Hickey... Writer will someday be in the arms of Dave Hickey, dead by the pool... Writer, did Writer have kids? Did Dave Hickey have kids? Writer never had kids... Who? Why couldn't Dave Hickey have had kids? if he'd had kids Writer could've been like him—been more like him... now he's not like him and Writer's not the same as him so Writer can't have anything to do with anything adjacent to him... that's literally insane... that's stupid, and insane... it's stupid, and yet, hm... there it is, stupid, and yet... the reader wants a break... the reader wants a break... give them more Céline breaks... *take a rest alongside that stupid anti-semite*... hm... *that racist moron... the dumb bubbling moron*... it's the present moment talking... it's any moment, it's any living moment talking... could there be transcendence in a pile of shit... sure, sure... could the one thing, the thing come together, sure... could the journey work, sure... could the death work, sure, of course... Céline knew how to layer his clothes well, though... from Céline Writer learned... Writer learned how to dress himself... no no... only from the other, there... there is the world, at dumb war with itself... a middling world commingled in its own shit with its smiley dipshit teeth... ah, yes, he'll stop it now... not yet, wait, no no... how hoary is your rasp... how ugly is your album... how great can your album be... how great can the albums of time be...

this being the crux of the argument surrounding the notion of freedom, then, Writer thinks… Writer doesn't know if there's a cowardice in seeking religion… Writer has had a difficult time with it… his friend once said "every day is the same," in this very resigned way, and it affected Writer and his wife quite a bit… Writer thinks there's truth to it, but remains determined that we do in fact make our lives as we live them, and thus the world we live in… people complain, sure, and must complain… so long as there is transcendence in their complaining, or not… either way, sure… Writer thinks there's a kind of proactive laziness too, that can be applied to the aspects of life we deem not as deserving our sincere attention than others… possibly and probably it's Writer deluding himself, and Writer simply possesses a general demeanor of optimism where some people see the opposite… no no… Writer hopes that there is some truth to it, sure… Writer doesn't think the notion of religiousness is particularly good or useful anymore, but there might be worth in the notion of god… at the very least the acknowledgment that God is not you… and thus there are aspects of life that Writer can simply decide might be beyond him… Writer guessed, and just guessed—or something like that… Writer finds the wearing of leather to be incredibly powerful… L.R.D.'s clothing, and not only their clothing, but their demeanor, their thin frames, the Ramones haircuts, the long bangs… there's something so powerful in it… the Telecaster, that machine, its living… the point of the machine is fuck you, or to say Writer's point to the machine to you is to say fuck you, the point being the fuck you, the you, the you of the diurnal, the demotic, the working day, fuck you…

whistles on the body… the SG, or Haino's, the leaning of them into whatever they were or were not doing… L.R.D. has a similar presence, a resignation… the band has a similar presence… no no… Writer liked listening and not understanding the words being sung, sure… a song could be about how pathetic Writer is, how fat and stupid Writer is, and Writer would have no idea, nor want one… it's difficult to think of how he's perceived here, now, being an American… there's something so stupid in being an American, and Writer thinks perhaps the world perceives Americans to be hopelessly stupid and dull… sure, yes… Writer does think the Americans are fundamentally a lazy people, being a human people, sure… Writer doesn't think that laziness is a negative attribute… Writer thinks if you can sit in the bathroom longer than you actually need to at work then you should do that… Writer thinks if you can avoid work by attending school ten years longer than might be necessary then you should do that… Writer thinks these are the small things in life that matter… Writer sees these terribly ambitious people, on all sides of society, everywhere… on one side it's realtors… on the other it's organic farmers… ambitious every one of them… Writer longed for them to simply take a nap, for the whole world to sleep… Writer received a rejection for a manuscript recently that hurt him, sure… he cried in the bathroom at work… Writer doesn't know what to do anymore… always tempted to quit… Writer doesn't know if it's just like suicidal ideation… Writer doesn't actually want in the present want to commit suicide, but the thought is there, and the thought is there for a reason, and Writer needs to figure out the reason if he was going to move beyond it… no no… Writer doesn't actually want to quit writing, no no… anything, yes, anything, can happen… the world wants to change, and so the person there will change it, with their forehead…

I must give you a piece of intelligence that you perhaps already know—namely, that the ungodly arch-villain Voltaire has died miserably like a dog—just like a brute. This is his reward! You must long since have remarked that I do not like being here, for many reasons, which, however, do not signify as I am actually here. I never fail to do my very best, and to do so with all my strength. Well, God will make all things right. I have a project in my head, for the success of which I daily pray to God. If it be His almighty will, it must come to pass; but, if not, I am quite contented. I shall then at all events have done my part. When this is in train, and if it turns out as I wish, you must then do your part also, or the whole work would be incomplete. Your kindness leads me to hope that you will certainly do so. Don't trouble yourself by any useless thoughts on the subject; and one favor I must beg of you beforehand, which is, not to ask me to reveal my thoughts more clearly till the time comes. It is very difficult at present to find a good libretto for an opera. The old ones, which are the best, are not written in the modern style, and the new ones are all good for nothing; for poetry, which was the only thing of which France had reason to be proud, becomes every day worse, and poetry is the only thing which requires to be good here, for music they do not understand. (Mozart)

Writer sat on the ground playing someone's piano, theirs… in the house by the forest in Japan… no, no… spending every day walking around looking for everything… going at night to wrestling events… going to their shows, any shows, anything… playing guitars, taking them apart on stage… meeting Moriaki Wakabayashi… no, no no… meeting no one, nobody… meeting the man with the primal scream… meeting with Janov in Chicago on the bus tossed into the sewer… Writer took the piano apart on the lawn with an ax… Writer won't look… Writer refused to look… Writer refused and Writer refused… Writer can't, way to fuck off… Writer can't wait to fuck off of earth… *O, if only instead of being a hell, the universe had been…* no no… somebody is on the TV… no no… all the time, everywhere— *she don't even know my name…* no no, a corpse… OK… this is not an entrance… *throughout my life I have seen, without one exception, narrow-shouldered men performing innumerable idiotic acts, brutalising their fellows, and corrupted souls by every means…* these are not entreaties, no no… the heater won't shut itself the fuck up… the heater won't stop its clanging… no—a radiator, it's a radiator… whatever it is it won't shut the fuck up… Writer can't wait for it to shut the fuck up… *do I hear twenty-one, twenty-*

one, twenty-one… I'll give you twenty-one, twenty-one, twenty-one… Willem Dafoe there dead upon the ground… sad, Italian corpse… Abel Ferrara being interviewed by Conan O'Brien seemingly drunk out of his skull… the staircase into the heavens, that man who'd hid within the coffin… no no… the forest, the forest is burning is Satan's church… no no… *I'll not be looking…* Writer woke up again inside the sun… Writer went out onto the surface of the sun to celebrate its perpetual rising… Writer felt lucky upon the sun… Writer felt very lucky… *My eyes were curled teeth…* Writer wasn't burned because Writer was within a thing… no no… *my body waffled, hither and yon…*

Writer welcomed in a good god… no no, any god, a dead god… whatever, no… Writer walked through a forest of burning material… his flesh was touched… one step, another… one step upon the sun, another… Writer woke up inside his own body… no no… his body herein therein whereon the sun, or no… the world peopled with burning… an humanity composed of shoulders… a hand upon the neighbor's shoulder, upon the sun… Writer quickly whittled a stick to knife… Writer split the root to hold his neck… to murder me… pissant hand on pissant hand… take her to the movies… she hasn't seen this one before… it's violent pornography… no no, Travis, don't… it's eaten, or Russian, or both… a query to the person sat within the theater's edge… a question, a… more of a comment than a question… a human question… a human certainty… a human document… a human rotting upon the floor within the church wherein Writer got fucked… Writer felt as though plopped upon the wood with splinters stuck into his flesh… Writer welcomed the discomfort of meetings, of gatherings… no no… cool, it's very cool of you to recognize that… it's very cool to remember the crimes he'd committed… a human personage within the bondage of an age of guilt… no no… everybody was facing the executioner, their executioner… thank God… as Writer has no question this person holds the secret for all the rest of us… that's not how you spell his name… Writer doesn't care… Writer can't be bothered to care… *one should let one's nails grow for a fortnight… no no… bring something incomprehensible into this world!*

while Writer understood the criticisms often lobbied at Zodiac signs and the like, his is likely to have as much bearing on who Writer became as anything else… no, no… it would make at least some level of sense that someone being born in June might dictate a variation in demeanor from someone born in December… and Writer thinks he feels this way and accepts this… no no… Writer was born as a Cancer because Writer was born when Writer was born… there are traits associated with Cancers that seem useful to engage when trying to engage whoever Writer is… again, as with the numerology, there are aspects Writer might recoil from, but it seems nevertheless worthwhile to consider the ways in which some website's accounting of the Zodiac's relationship to whoever Writer wound up becoming—and yes it's annoying to refer to him this way, and alas no it won't stop… *shut the fuck up!* house, second riff…

Fitzgerald contrasts rupture with structural pseudobreaks in so-called signifying chains. But he also distinguishes it from more supple, more subterranean links or stems of the "voyage" type, or even from molecular conveyances. "The famous 'Escape' or 'run away from it all' is an excursion in a trap even if the trap includes the South Seas, which are only for those who want to paint them or sail them. A clean break is something you cannot come back from; that is irretrievable because it makes the past cease to exist." Can it be that voyages are always a return to rigid segmentarity? Is it always your daddy and mommy that you meet when you travel, even as far away as the South Seas, like Melville? Hardened muscles? Must we say that supple segmentarity itself reconstructs the great figures it claimed to escape, but under the microscope, in miniature? Beckett's unforgettable line is an indictment of all voyages: "We don't travel for the fun of it, as far as I know; we're foolish, but not that foolish." (D & G)

this was a very odd time in Writer's living… Writer worried about the past… it's very odd to know that we don't understand this thing that is always happening and is oftentimes very disconcerting… no no… Writer worries about his life, his money, his marriage… Writer doesn't know if God is the word for this sort of thing… Writer is quite dumb… Writer does not mind being made fun of… Writer doesn't like much recent stuff, or it's maybe all Writer really likes… Writer loved to hide in libraries… something else, somewhere, controls it… psychic mold, oops… Writer gets sickly if Writer finds he's taken in a bit of mold… or even mold-adjacent matter… being so direct seems very stupid though… Writer doesn't know if this will be the last work, it surely could, Writer thinks… saying that though feels very stupid… OK… Writer is just incredibly dumb… Writer likes to watch television or videos on his iPhone on YouTube that Writer opens and then moves around so that Writer can partially watch the videos on his iPhone on YouTube and partially do a lot of other things… OK… Writer has even published them, his histories… no no… Stel Igil Dahl, is that how it's spelled?

Writer doesn't look at these aspects of the animal kingdom with disdain or judgment… a long time to listen to music and to think… Writer doesn't do well when it comes to speaking to people, with people… in his case if anything the opposite has been true… Writer's wife saw one when they went camping recently and Writer didn't feel compelled to run from it, just sort of stand there and stare, dumbly… Writer tried to be better than his father, whatever that actually means… Writer remembered going to this bookstore in downtown Spokane near the Target Writer would buy cereal at… you're repeating yourself… Writer is always fucking things up… Writer has to say that Writer doesn't think Writer does, for the most part, believe in this… his mom had left at this point, Writer thinks, no… Writer's mother was there, Writer thinks, and Writer saw her, Writer thinks, but no, perhaps not… Writer doesn't really expect to be told the truth about anything either, which may go back to his parents, he isn't sure… no no… Writer doesn't want people to be able to work, or need to… Writer read some of it and now it's in his…

alone in his office on campus, no no… in the office of the gas station… no, at work… no no… at the gas station in the forest… Writer can't imagine it, and Writer doesn't want to, and Writer doesn't think about this sort of thing ever… Writer has had periods of days, weeks, or months when Writer couldn't take care of things because Writer couldn't move, couldn't get going…

people are too reductive about the notion of hatred… OK… being someone who hates could potentially be a good thing… perhaps… love is an overrated thing… OK… the world is full of love… sure… love has made this world… hatred is the belief that love has failed this world… could that be true… people are too reductive about love… Writer was embarrassed to have misspelled the name, something… however, Writer believes Writer has come too far to turn back now… no no… the little idiot sits upon the stool and paints a picture of his home… his limbs skirt and dawdle upon the paper… the small fool… OK… the paper covers the sheet… the sheet covers the room… their images cover the paint… *my body there upon the floor… my dumb body upon the floor in the center of the living room…* hatred is purity… it said that somewhere, maybe on a church… painted, no no… a book can be a sacred item, at least Writer thought that once, in that video game… he's had a rough go of things… *I'm drinking from a 1 GAL jug of Arizona Diet Green Tea with Ginseng…* Writer poured some sparkling water in there… no no, ice… and some Crystal Light with some green tea… Writer, dieting… Writer, been dieting for months now, failing to… Writer, the lowest he's been in years and still he's pretty fat… Writer carries it all in his gut… his humors, there… Writer only ever carried all of it in his gut… the body is putrid… the arms and legs are skinny and not muscular… no no… Writer carries all of the fat in his chest and gut… no no… Writer looks like a cartoon butler or something…

no no… Writer doesn't look good, doesn't look OK, doesn't look well… the facial hair is not attractive… Writer doesn't brush his teeth enough… Writer looks like Wilburn Burchette, or Peter Brötzmann, or Herman Melville, in that one picture—at least he does with a long beard, an ugly beard… Writer doesn't shower enough… Writer used to shower plenty… Writer doesn't bathe enough… Writer, gross, pretty gross—Writer is living an atypical life, homeschooled children, becoming a person, having a family, talking to a bunny—talking to the chickens, being alone with the family around him, living outside of the world, but trapped in it… Writer, an ugly dog, an ugly man... Writer, the body is an ugly vitamin thing... the vitamins smell bad... Writer, freebasing the vitamins... Writer, an American... Writer, a boy, a little boy, a frightened little boy... Rick Moranis took time off to be with his wife... was she sick? once, one time, Writer awakening in the shrine of resurrection... Writer living in a video game... Writer, watching Survivor... Writer loves Jeff Probst... Writer carried the computer across the room... no no... Writer picked it up on its side... a person is wearing a white outfit and they look like the leader of a cult... Writer, the leader of the world's smallest cult, and they don't believe in anything... *I'm listening to something in my right ear, and nothing in my left ear... I'm not listening to any music...* a film is playing... no no... a record... no, it's a film... Let Sleeping Corpses Lie... no no... Come My Fanatics... no no... the Wizard in Black... *you're all the same the lot of you...*

if Writer were listening to that music Writer thinks this might be easier, working this way... Writer saw Electric Wizard performing... within a city, upon a stage... a video was playing behind them, a weird quasi-pornographic witch thing... the video cut and it said something dumb, like INPUT, with a blue screen behind the band performing... a fan tried to tell them what had happened, and the singer, gave him the finger and screamed FUCK YOU... Writer liked to let the ellipses run... Writer had no idea whether a reader would feel anything about them... it's Writer's belief that a writer should think about a reader, though this hasn't always been Writer's belief... Writer believes a lot of things... his teeth are silver... every tooth in his stupid pathetic mouth is silver... his breasts are violent... his teeth are silvery violent... Writer got a copy of the book the people they're talking about... you know the book... whoever you are, wherever you are in your life, you know the one... what a gigantic piece of shit we've made of living... isn't it simply wonderful? isn't it the most wonderful thing within the world? a body sits within a room... no no... a person has that body... someone has that body... it's important... it's so incredibly important... it's obvious how incredibly important it is to every single person living... the Oscars, the Oscars... people like to talk about the Oscars... Will Smith slapped L. Ron Hubbard's reanimated corpse in the face, across the face, upon the stage... Writer loved the texture of it—the sheet, not that sheet, the mattressed sheet... someone slapped someone... a famous millionaire slapped a famous millionaire... you can't get enough of it... you love to see it all... shave your head... drive in your Subaru Crosstrek from 2014... drive and get excited about the music that's playing—it's L.R.D.... a wonderful song... a wonderful whispering woeful thing... a screaming violent song... a band is playing a screaming violent muted whispery non-song...

apparently within the study of numerology Writer is positioned along the path of 1... no no... this is sort of adjacent to the Zodiac stuff that Writer has also been exploring... the path of 1 is tied to a sort of initiative, a drive, a determination to figure things out on one's own… no no… it's difficult with these things because reading something like "born leader" Writer couldn't feel any more alienated from the path of 1, or humanity… Writer doesn't like to lead, and never has… he's sort of headstrong about some things, but usually employed this headstrongness in a passive aggressive internal dialogue that's occasionally pronounced and erupts when he's alone… Writer guessed it made a certain level of sense in terms of his work, but the self-deprecating nature Writer inherited in being from the church made him cringe in apology when reading this stuff that's supposedly about him… no no… anger alone and in the car… being born in the church is probably significant, and Washington in particular… no no… although Washington has grown in stature, basically entirely resulting from the success or failure of musician X and his efforts as creator of the project XXXXX… for much of his life Writer, for much of Writer's life the notion that Writer was from Washington was sort of resented… Writer wanted to be from a more interesting place, and the people who seemed to really relish being from Washington—in youth it was a substitute teacher with an aw shucks demeanor, now it's XXXXX and all that that entails—put him off quite a bit… Writer now lives in a similar quiet place to the place Writer grew up, in the wilderness away from the gas station, the forest… Writer guessed maybe Writer hoped it will remain what it presently is, but Writer doesn't care anymore, and

Washington is a fine place, and the people, perhaps especially those just mentioned, are fine people… anger alone and in the car—anger alone and in the car…

time, of late, seemed to be moving faster, and it's only been through highly artificial structural apparatuses that Writer has been able to feel anything but this seemingly inexhaustible movement forward, where Writer takes in too much information for any of it to have shape, definition—and the sense of a vague impending doom is always around… when Writer decided to work on this project, and to do something similar to what he'd tried to do with another group of musicians, Writer was walking, in Washington—late at night—and listening to *The OZ Tapes*, having looked back into L.R.D. for the first time in a couple of months, and realizing they'd recently released material with the passing of T.M… X, no no… on this walk Writer communicated with Editor, Writer then listened to the entirety of the album twice, watched videos of the band, and Writer started to write down ideas… Writer knew he wanted to call this book whatever it's presently being called… no no… Writer knew that he needed to figure out how to write a book about a band that's barely lent their words to anything in any capacity beyond the declaration made by a group of terrorists the bassist—and possibly someone else, the singer? founder? T.M.? X? it's vague enough—was a part of, having to do with a popular manga focusing on a boxer… no no… they didn't want to write about themselves, and possibly they don't want to be written about at all, so how do you write a book like that? How do you attempt to write about a band whose members are like B. Traven? Bolaño's only approach to addressing B. Traven came in the form of fiction, more or less... *shut up*... his fiction edged close too reality... *ohmygodshutup*... Aira writes from reality, and both feel connected to Stanislaw Lem, who wrote imaginary ideas for books and reviews of same while also writing slim works of science fiction that could then be adapted into spiritual films by Andrei Tarkovsky—the house burning, in two films the footage of a burning house, it's perfect... *seriouslypleaseshutthefuckup*... there are connections, then, to be had, or made, or drawn...

fiction of late draws more and more from actual life... *shutthefuckupyoufuckingbaby*... the notion of autofiction seems a bit dead, though, in terms of writing grandly about one's own life... *thisissofuckingboring*... critifiction, then, which Writer... *quiet, Opleasebequiet*... so a work about a band that doesn't want to be written about written by a writer conceiving of the project as a fictive thing even while writing short responsive passages to various writers as a jumping off point to discussing the band... no no... sure—sure, try it... Writer guessed it was attemptable... no no... maybe too the same press could put the book out... no no... sure, no... so we are bound by these structures of time, and forced to figure out what they're going to do to make our lives meaningful... one day we'll be able to distinguish among ten, twenty, or thirty-thousand different noises… the past is alive, as this raw nerve, or a broken piece of electronics swinging over a puddle… that's how the past feels for Writer, a thing that can cause harm, harm him—a place where he made endless mistakes and fucked up as a human being… Writer the human being… even now Writer regrets not publishing under his entire name… *Writer*… it seems more distinguished somehow…

A Writer is one who imposes silence on this speech and a literary work is, for one who knows how to penetrate it, a rich resting place of silence, a firm defense and a high wall against this eloquent immensity that addresses us by turning away from ourselves. If, in this imaginary Tibet, where the sacred sign could no longer be discovered in anyone, all literature stopped speaking, what would be lacking is silence, and it is this lack of silence that would perhaps reveal the disappearance of literary language. (Blanchot)

too late now, yes yes… Writer the human making endless mistakes and being a kind of a piece of shit… then having a child… then being a piece of shit some more… then trying to deal with things a bit… no no… then being anxious about the past… then the OCD, the depression, the anxiety, the addiction, everything… sure, no no… the future, too, is scary… no no… it's like a gate, into this kind of heavenly place, but Writer knows the figure from *Mulholland Drive* is hiding somewhere, ready to jump out and fuck up his entire sense of things…

me, imagining that Thou, O Lord God, the Truth, wert a vast and bright body, and I a fragment of that body... the present, this is the thing Writer would like to direct attention towards... it's no surprise why so much of AA is directed towards staying in today, in this moment... the addict or alcoholic is doing this by accident in active addiction... as long as there's a drug or a drink or even just a vaguely fucked up experience to work towards and chase then that works pretty well, living thusly... you sober up and what, you sober up and all you can think about is every stupid thing you've ever done... you get sober and for a time you feel pretty great, but anxieties about the past and future, which you used drugs and drink to escape entirely, now come back infected, poisoned so they're all you can fixate on... temporalities, then, become a horror show... over and over, then, in meetings, you're told to stay in today, and it's helpful... no no... Writer thinks, even, Writer thinks even though it's not consistently effective... perhaps the art of the past is a means of looking into it without completely spiraling... the future, too, if contextualized in terms of art we might make, or read, or listen to, could similarly help us to deal... the present, then, becomes the issue, the only issue—the only concern... no no... you have to turn your focus into things you can actually conceive of, or touch... listening to an album... taking a walk... deciding to write a book about a band... don't eat too much... unless it's fruit... drink some water... maybe coffee... sit and exist in a state of relative discipline and see... New York City is fine...

or not... you don't live in that world... the world within the world is the world here... the state... the dead rain in Washington... the snow in Japan... your bodies on the ground in the night, stoned or not, looking up... people existing together and living within living within the world... walking some more... sitting to write a bit of this book in the middle of your day while your child sits next to you... trying to create and conceive of objectives... problems, creating problems—proofs... giving yourself meaning... giving meaning meaning... this, too, is another reason the constant talking about the worthlessness, or uselessness, of art, bothers Writer... it's possible that when Oscar Wilde said it—*wrote it* (?)—there might've been truth to it, but when Writer sits down and reads something, or watches a film, or listens to an album, the notion of it being meaningless, or useless, or worthless, couldn't be further from his mind... tell a football fan about the uselessness of football... tell an elementary school art teacher that art is useless, while a room full of kids make small paintings to look like windows... it's an extension of the existential position, that life is meaningless, that there's no inherent meaning to what we do, but going forward if someone wants to talk about the unnecessary of art, they should be required to expand from this, and make a solid case that nothing matters, and then maybe they could talk about why books, films, albums, all of it has no meaning—is unnecessary, doesn't matter, is worthless, useless, whatever else... sure, OK, sure... Writer thinks we are doomed to the reality that this stuff does matter… it's easier to think that it doesn't, that nothing matters… it's easy, nihilism is easy, pessimism is easy—this is the thing… if it doesn't matter, if nothing matters, then we're off the hook… the reality, though, is that unfortunately for human being is that it matters, just like the past and present do, and it's no less valid to go forward thinking whatever matters to you actually does matter, and that that's a positive thing, and that should be explored… the default position of nihilism is the easiest thing in the world… it's like the irony thing, this sense that we can all kind of roll our eyes at life, at living, and that this is *cool*, and that we should do this and try not to look like we *care*, that we *try*, that we're interested… we're frightened because this is the stupid dynamic of life, and our efforts to push against it are probably more important now than they've ever been, though we could have said this at any time in history…

someone somewhere is being racist… no no… someone, some American is being a piece of shit… someone else is being told it's in them, it's what they are—this piece-of-shit-ness… there are the pieces of shit, the profound rotund pieces of shit… here are the pieces of shit, the ambling navel-gazing pieces of shit… here are the young men, the world on their shoulders… here is the hung neck of Ian Curtis in his home… how long was Writer there before Deborah Curtis discovered him… Writer was in the house, floating there? how is it possible that his work was completed when he was just twenty-three years old? no no… Writer means what, Writer means—Writer knows technically it wasn't completed, probably… no no… but that begs the question, if someone ends something with such finality—their life—aren't they sort of saying they're done? no no… they're sort of saying they're done, but only sort of… OK… lots of people choose to kill themselves… Curtis was one… apparently Curtis was interested in doing more in the realm of dub, or reggae, of embracing his fondness for Genesis P-Orridge… *stop it*… Writer can see what—see that… *he wasn't there*… Writer can hear it… *no he can't*… New Order doesn't seem to have—New Order doesn't seem like it continued in that spirit… they did something else… Writer wants to like them much more than Writer in fact does… bad cocaine music… maybe *The Pale King* is sort of finished, right… *don't say "right" like that after every tiny thing you say—like an asshole*… Writer means, in terms of the work that particular author felt capable of completing, it is sort of finished… it's sad, and everything is sad… of course it's sad… a person ends their life… there are sadder things, but suicide is there, it's up there, it's horrid… a person kills themselves… *I'm sorry, I'm so sorry*… Writer does think it's possible to think of the works left when a person commits suicide as being finished… you sound like you're being patronizing… Gilles Deleuze jumped out of a window after a battle with respiratory illness… Gilles Deleuze is dead… a lot of people don't feel like that…

Writer hasn't read what's left behind by anyone... not all of it anyway... we're gonna play tennis soon, or pickle ball... he's a really good tennis player... that's one of the things that's amazing to someone... he's a wonderful athlete... you have to go to the top of a hill with the big rock person... you have to help them hide as you scale the rock... it's nice to think of the ways in which this is exactly like the first example, the first iteration, of it... prior to this, this document contained two-thousand-six-hundred-and-sixty-six words... now it contains more... and more still... Writer never finished that book... Writer liked *The Savage Detectives* more... Writer guessed it's OK to talk about this kind of thing in a project like his... *this is a novel,* if Writer says so—says it is... a novella? sorry to the reader as this paragraph isn't going to stop until the book stops... no no, that isn't true... the ellipses do what, offer what—hopefully offer a bit of respite... *do they...* Writer hopes they do... Writer likes to break up a sentence... Writer likes to break it up... too scared to break it up now... just too frightened... people are talking about fucking on the podcast... your body is coffee, caffeine—coffee, coffee, coffee... your coffee is there upon the beach ball... you're where—she doesn't exist... that woman doesn't exist... good luck, good riddance, I'm watching a film now—no no... maybe though you do, or your grandmother does... Writer can't wait to move to Florida when he's old... he's going to watch so much television when he's old... Writer completely understands why people move there when they're old... what a wonderful way to live one's life… Writer thinks if he's able to Writer might move there sooner… he'd like that quiet… Writer can't wait to be old, except for the defecation… Writer can't imagine the defecation for an older person is much in the way of pleasure… he'd like to be wrong… now he's probably at his peak in terms of defecation, and it's not good… Writer can't remember what it felt like to defecate when he was younger… Writer remembers the anxiety—being anxious about it—though… Writer wondered a lot lately about how Writer can't remember the first time he'd had an orgasm… it seemed insane to him, that Writer could've done this thing, such a drastic thing—almost painful—and then not remember it as this almost kind of traumatic event… alright, stop… we will not have to imitate these noises but rather to combine them according to our artistic fantasy… the discography with care… can't language…

Writer doesn't want to talk about that shit so much anymore, or anything—at all—ever… no no… Writer just doesn't want to… Writer thinks talking about it in books and novels and the like is sort of cliché… Writer thinks there's just more stuff a person can write about… beyond the bedroom wall, beyond anything, beyond New York City, beyond being cool, beyond Paris, beyond the internet, beyond sophistication… no no… Writer thinks it's important to try and write more about other things… *you tell me it calms your nerves*… the commas there Writer doesn't enjoy—*where?* Writer was going to do full stop periods but that seemed dramatic…

OK... people have to try... man—so awful... so awful in that Fugazi documentary... knowing—on looking—America's gone a saggy straight and... the fans don't even know what band they're seeing... just 90s people using it as an excuse to get high and fuck off... the band couldn't be more sort of against that spirit... however therein lies a problem, of course... the band is of this spirit that they're not against any spirit—*they are, though*—but Writer does think that Jem Cohen is sort of making the case that they might be against that particular spirit, which is a negative, unhelpful spirit—*because they are too*... hmm... it's unhelpful to just fuck off out of life... Writer likes that band, though... not talking about Fugazi, that other band... Writer likes that band Uncle Acid and the Deadbeats... that's a spirit Writer can enjoy... the same spirit Writer guessed Writer would argue that Big L operated in, or L.R.D.... and even though he'd watched Ian Mackaye talk about how he can't fathom making gangster rap and promoting this sort of violence or nihilism, no no—Writer contains that... Writer walks to his car after work and Writer listens to Big L and Writer feels that spirit... Uncle Acid and the Deadbeats, on "I'll Cut You Down," they say *I was born a wicked man/no hopes or dreams/I get my kicks from torturing and screams*... no no... it's evil... is it an evil sentiment? something about it compels Writer... Writer is not actually drawn to the reality of that lived violence, but the spirit of being sort of antinomian... OK... at least it's his belief that this sort of thing is antinomian... being sort of against the everyday, that sort of thing, the conventional, that sort of thing, sure… just, I—sandwich, sandwiche, sandwiches… Writer didn't much enjoy that one book that was very long—which was very long—and contained largely one sentence… Writer did however enjoy that other one book which—*that*—was very long and contained largely one sentence—one *different* sentence… this one will be shorter, which is probably a selling point—though Writer has to accept that he's never really written anything that could be sold—which could, or would, be sold… a night in Snoqualmie, Washington… a night when the sun is setting there… on the floor are Legos… in varied piles—no no, Duplos, on the floor the Duplos in varied piles… elsewhere is a podcast and a Nickelodeon TV show about monster trucks that turn into other things… OK—which… Writer doesn't think it's the thing you immediately thought of when Writer said that, though—which… piss upon the floor and run away… drive a truck made of bones—sure, sure… check your email… write an email to your dead dad… no no—he's not—he isn't dead… great—no… Writer loves it—this—which… incredibly stupid purple prose… feeling so stupid—feeling so incredibly stupid…

take a shower—take a bath—read Scott Bradfield… don't listen to them—don't let the world go away… or do—piss upon the milk upon the pissy floor—milk-plus… living in the wilder-… no no—not the wilderness, no… great—another book… another godforsaken book—a godforsaken book printed there... a little room in hell—the glassy part... sure, OK—OK... the frozen part of hell—the frozen part of hell that—which—nobody talks about... Satan frozen there upon some kind of throne... Writer pictures it in space, in total darkness, a total void... everything impossibly cold—the human suffering there being febrile—a true hell, containing not just the refuse of human being, but other species? Aliens? *shutthefuckup*... in what capacity are the hostages housed—describe it... at which point along the route to hell do they find themselves within... no, no—the route to hell is the same from every place... it's difficult to think of the worst thing in the world... perhaps it is being beheaded and having it shared on the internet... no no... perhaps it is being maimed in the name of something shiny... no no... perhaps it is being defiled upon a splintery wooden floor... no no... whatever it is has nothing to do with writers... with Writer—whatever it is has nothing to do with hair... maybe not—no no... it's tough to know where to put one's energy... put it into something either living or dying... we invest in lots of dumb endeavors... perhaps the investment inaugurates its dumbness, brings it about... no no... is it a shawarma onto which a lot of lamb is put? is that the word for that device? and what of the questions without question marks... Writer could easily get very interested in firearms... sure—any American could do it... of that Writer has no doubt... Writer thinks a lot about the second Indiana Jones film, picture... lines from it echo through his skull... combs—too many comes—*whogivesashit*... when

Writer was young Writer tried to rap… no no—its embarrassing—it's too embarrassing… he loved the music… Writer loved, and still loves, Project Pat… the same as the Writer understood, what hurt it is, if a man understands what Thou, the light of all true-speaking minds… Writer loved an evilness, an antinomianness there, and wasn't cool, and had no idea who L.R.D. might be, or might've been—wasn't cool—then… there's nothing as embarrassing as a person's entire life…

here Writer is, naked in Manhattan, being flogged— no no… ah so you've finally made your way through *The Mad Man; or, the Mysteries of Manhattan*… is that how the title goes? is that how it ends? Writer is never sure—it's Melvillian… or Melvilleian… is it Melvilleian to attend a sex club? sure, sure… a leather bar? sure… that sort of thing… was Melville's house really filled up with young men to do his work? who said that… Paul Metcalf? Melville and Hawthorne rolling around on the floor of a barn while a cow sits there idly chewing its cud… no no… the calm at the end of the day—a real peacefulness… and is Melville a terrible father and does this make Writer a terrible father—being, being… is it the cud it chews? Writer is never sure… Paul Metcalf was doing what, exactly, and when—when did he work—and where, and did he labor in the same misery as all of us—and did he watch TV… a Ferris Wheel upon the scream… no no… personalize your screensaver… OK… did you know—Prime members have free unlimited photo storage with Amazon photos… OK—no no… not now—get started… a waterfall gives way to a field—possibly a moor… sure, a moor—a moot moor… a moor run amok amorously mooting its physical body… no no—the moors murders—no no…

Primitive people attributed to sound a divine origin. It became surrounded with religious respect, and reserved for the priests, who thereby enriched their rites with a new mystery. Thus was developed the conception of sound as something apart, different from and independent of life. The result of this was music, a fantastic world superimposed upon reality, an inviolable and sacred world. This hieratic atmosphere was bound to slow down the progress of music, so the other arts forged ahead and bypassed it. The Greeks, with their musical theory mathematically determined by Pythagoras, according to which only some consonant intervals were admitted, have limited the domain of music until now and made almost impossible the harmony they were unaware of. In the Middle Ages music did progress through the development and modifications of the Greek tetracord system. But people kept considering sound only in its unfolding through time, a narrow conception so persistent that we still find it in the very complex polyphonies of the Flemish composers. The chord did not yet exist; the development of the different parts was not subordinated to the chord that these parts could produce together; the conception of these parts was not vertical, but merely horizontal. The need for and the search for the simultaneous union of different sounds (that is to say of its complex, the chord), came gradually: the assonant common chord was followed by chords enriched with some random dissonances, to end up with the persistent and complicated dissonances of contemporary music. (Russolo)

Bataille writing on *Wuthering Heights*... was that the work... the immorality of literature... on immoral literature... Writer can't finish it... Writer gets to sit in the room in his body once again... Writer likes to put a sound on—a noise on... the music made by the hand—the band—or by Shizuka... how mortifying it is to be young—to age—to be old... a person—just think of it... a welcome home—the body... Writer would like to live in a cemetery... or just above one, tending to it... not being melodramatic... doesn't that seem like a peaceful prospect for a body... graveyard clay—the dirty dust—no no... whatever it is... that Irishman—the other one—the political one... a violence undertaken by mankind—you go mankind... Writer liked to watch the people making fun of one another... Writer liked to billow out like a fat bloated cloud—bleating... good morning, fuckface! good afternoon, fuckface! good evening, fuckface! hey there, fuckface! good night, fuckface! Writer, glad to hover around the counter with his friend whose grandparents' kitchen looked like the one in the YouTube video that's always being recommended to him... no no... Writer, looking forward to playing the song "White Waking" in a minute, again, for—Writer thinks—the fourth time today... once your wife and your body or your family or a snow cone drove around that city where the people lived to try and see how they lived and it felt bad but your wife liked it and you felt it was this big secret you could be a part of and share and this meant something more to you than the little things you've sort of amassed as talismans around your living and there's such warmth to it that it's difficult to think of anything better than that… your wife, and you, doing something maybe slightly illegal—or strange—and this binding you together, forever… sometimes writers romanticize criminals, or being a certain way, or whatever else, and the only thing you can respond to it with is you're right, but you're a fucking calendar… when Writer shot Jesse James Writer was sixty-four years old on an island in the South Pacific and Writer had gout and Writer came into town and put a knife to the throat of a young man there and Writer walked up to him and stuck his head under his arm so that the knife went to and through Writer's own neck and Writer shot through the top of his skull then—Jesse James'—from his underchin and both of them there perished upon the sand-swept path…

Writer can't wait until they make Flamin' Hot Diet Mountain Dew—perhaps it's already been done—you can't keep up… it has—has it… Writer's wife and Writer did the one chip challenge and it just felt like they were bad people for half an hour… no no… Writer being Kit Carson—no, Kim Carson—no no… in the red night… on the dead road… and young William is there—the western land—the boy, on speed and near death… and Joan Vollmer is there, a bit drunk, and with a bullethole in the center of her face… for several days Writer has been trying to figure out what to spend a small amount of money on… no no—you can't—you oughtn't… Writer will convince himself he's got the thing, but then convince himself Writer doesn't need it… over and over this happens—it happens; is happening—which is probably something, though Writer doesn't have any interest in figuring out what it is—like when Bandini sits on the bed and eats a big bag of oranges, with no desire to go anywhere, with no desire to do anything… OK—OK… let Writer sit in the corner of the room and try to figure out where Writer hid the pliers—fetch the pliers… OK—welcome to Hazelden good morning here's a folder here's some other shit here's some other other shit… Writer needs to take the phone—bring it… Writer needs to eat a phone—it's time… a good morning phone, the morning phone… good, holding onto the phone… O that's wonderful another nine-hundred-page novel… O that's wonderful a book that has nothing to do with the world… O that's wonderful a novel that has nothing to do with Megan Thee Stallion… O that's wonderful a book being published by a publisher that's paid for every single review… did anyone even write the reviews… Writer doesn't like to see the men… renditions of the theme music from *Ocarina of Time* on Alexa—the theme at night in Gerudo Valley, where no men live… a phone on the couch… show—show you—like, in same speak... cityspeak... that speak... imagine calling yourself a transcendentalist... Harald Grosskopf living alone painting himself silver... *dammit uh enough Americans—if make—more, the...*

this is how Writer feels... Writer doesn't know what Writer feels about life—this information—exactly how someone like Sartre felt, but Writer does think it's a useful conception for a human life—*what is?*—when opposed to any conception of life after death... sure, OK... Writer thinks this is another area wherein he's fundamentally opposed to most religious thinking... Writer doesn't think life after death exists, because it doesn't seem to make any sense... Writer doesn't want a system of belief that treats human beings as different from other living things, and most of them are tied to this... the people who developed these ideas about an eternal life were facing such horrible odds, horrible lives... starving, diseased, thirsty to the point of hallucination, so they develop a mindset around the idea that life on earth is the horror we endure for a good life thereafter... and people have taken that and brought it into our lives even though there are millions upon millions of people who, when compared with the average person living two or three thousand years ago, are living like kings... but still people held onto eternal life... why would anyone hope to live any longer than human being already lives? Writer wouldn't even want to live as long as those massive centuries-old whales... eternal life? are you an idiot? it takes like twenty years for a person to do enough fucked-up stuff to saddle them with guilt for the rest of their days, but people really want to live forever? people are the dumbest living things in the universe… dumber than dumb stupid chickens… dumber than sap… dumber than the skunks and the raccoons… dumber than shrimp… dumber than Bill Maher… dumber than worms… dumber than bugs… dumber than dogs… dumber than all cats… dumber than trout… dumber than all fish… dumber than coral… dumber than shit… dumber than tacks… people are just so fucking stupid… and they're creeps… and they're idiots… and they die, and that's it… and I'm leading the pack… go to any Buffalo Wild Wings… sit there for two hours, eating a full meal, watching a game, eating some dessert… look around that room and imagine spending an eternity with those people… imagine the horror—how horrible that would be… think about how horrible that would be… now multiply it infinitely and imagine some massive world containing all people ever… just get real… just for the sake of anything get real, won't you? just think about it and just get real… Writer does think there's a presence here of L.R.D. in the ongoingness of what L.R.D. mastered… no no… shut up… Writer thinks that there are artforms that welcome a sense of constancy, the constant… OK… books that don't really follow any grand trajectory… commonplace books… diaries—the diary… diaries might be the great unsung literary form for this… Writer will start another diary—a diary—again… no no… Robert Shields' being perhaps—Robert Shields' diary perhaps being the best example, as he's so concerned with diurnal matters that the only sense of starting and finishing—from the pages Writer has been able to read—the entire thing won't be available for some time—from the—is whenever you start looking at any portion of it and whenever you decide to stop… that's it… Writer once talked with a friend who makes music about the notion of making an album that would take a year to listen to… no no… Writer doesn't know whether this would mean people would listen, and then stop, and then resume exactly where they'd stopped, where they were—or if they'd listen to fragments here and there, hither and yon… Writer liked that, though… maybe encourages psychedelic reissue—about— around…

Beethoven and Wagner for many years wrung our hearts. But now we are sated with them and derive much greater pleasure from ideally combining the noise of streetcars, internal-combustion engines, automobiles, and bust crowds than from rehearsing, for example, the 'Eroica' or the 'Pastorale'…away! … be gone, since we shall not much longer succeed in restraining a desire to create a new musical realism by a generous distribution of sonorous blows and slaps, leaping numbly over violins, pianofortes, contrabasses, and groaning organs, Away! (Russolo)

Neu Products Era

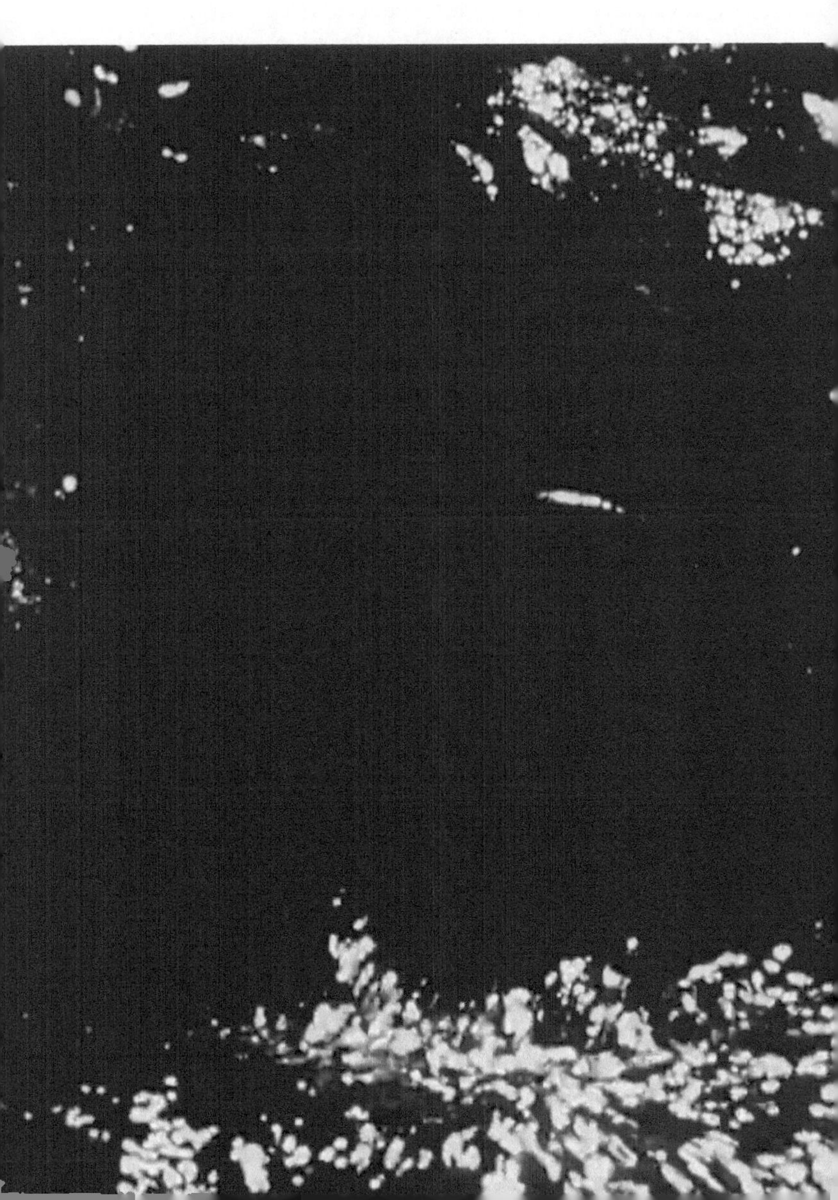

Writer has begun thinking of certain forms of music—*writing*—as ambient, even if—and especially if, let's say—they weren't necessarily intended as such... the Grateful Dead were the first example that struck him... birdsong... their satellite radio station, because you might listen in to a portion of a live show in Kentucky in 1986, and return later to hear the album version of "Uncle John's Band," and return still later to hear a recording from a festival in France in 1977... no no... and each of these iterations feel connected, like they could be laid out side by side without issue... OK—on top of one another or in a sprawl, the writing a kind of quilting, the musicking a kind of quilting... then black metal, with its atypical song structures—*are they?*—ambient outside instruments that create a sort of oppressive heaping, and longer albums which might feature field recordings—or simply *be* field recordings— random bits of piano or synthesizer, and other forms of music on top of the loud, droning, abrasive guitars and vocals... even the burial of instruments or clothing before gigs... this could contribute to the sound... and the loud braying of L.R.D.'s recorded sets filled with everything possible, every stitch of feedback, everything weeping and wet with rain... Sunn O))) distilled this masterfully with *Kannon*, where the practice of droning is done with guitars that sound plucked from Mayhem's first album... Mick Barr, too, has done incredible things with this... Writer can't say enough good about Mick Barr... Mick Barr and L.R.D. and that would be sufficient... in Writer's opinion Mick Barr is the greatest guitarist alive—who ever lived... and then L.R.D., which might be the pinnacle of ambience because if you listen to all of the releases presently available you'll find contradictions in terms of song parts, and tracks that might well have been played for minutes before the recording you're listening to picked up... the music, too, feels like a blending of black metal ideas with the Grateful Dead's approach to performing, and recording their stuff... it's pop— it's noise—but it's intentional noise, with singing that feels profoundly intimate, loving, almost too close—with bass and guitar parts that, when the wall of sound is sort of cut through, might be taken from '50s or '60s bubblegum pop records... it's incredible that this exists—that the work exists—and more incredible that—considering the band's apparent ideas regarding presence, fame, art, distribution, transmission—what remains is sufficient to extract these components and put the puzzle back together into something truly captivating...

Writer's anxiety is a part of the project—this project... his medication is a part of this project—the project, the overall project, the apparatus—the Venlavaxine, the Amitriptyline, whatever else... Writer's anxiety is part and parcel with the measly mound he's attempted to construct in the name of someone X... Writer's uncertain of the rest—all of it... his name is not the public name and no matter how many times Writer sifts through blood Writer still feels the glint of suffering and smiles back when the world has said its piece... Writer's father was a miserable man...

is this where it comes from? Writer's mother was what… Writer's father the cabin, alone—unacabine, a hole…

Writer's mother the walking, the beach… both equally somewhere, on the ground and in the earth—somewhere, in Washington, living together, not coming apart, not splitting, not what… both just as American as every living soul… good riddance to old rubbish, or no… Writer, writhing… Writer, sifted through countless speeches and those two somehow seemed essential—what, *what*—no no… Writer has plagiarized in the name of, of what… Writer has plagiarized in the face of an abjection, of abject failure and suffering at the hands of the academy… no no—*what*… Writer has written countless dissertations… Writer has written the beginnings of countless dissertations… no no… you sit down and you write is how it happens… Writer has written about the Inca and their methods of calculation… sure, OK… Writer has written about Howard Hughes and imagined infected wounds where he'd had his morphine injected… yes, yes… Writer has written about Mother Teresa meeting with Christopher Hitchens and both of them sweating and nervous and pathetic… no no… none of it so swelled Writer's chest against the infinite as this—the buried noises of everyday life—*which one is pathetic, Mother Teresa or Hitchens? You can't talk like that—not now, not ever*—fine, Hitchens, per Leys, per whatever his real name is—*fine*—was she good? *I don't know*… the work of L.R.D. the perfect music of what—the perfect music of the ground, beneath the ground, living within the rotting ground there below… forming, deforming, fungal… Sade taking his prisoners and having them perform acts that metaphorized the very acts as they were performed, in turn reassembled in Italy on the coast or so just a throw or a sniff from where—*they weren't his prisoners*—the wording is confusing but yes they were… no no… we've seen the work… Hitchcockian, maybe… *Salo; or, the 120 Days of Sodom,* directed by Alfred Hitchcock, starring James Mason… no no… atop a piano? what of noises in cinema? what of it? the humming in *Stalker,* the humming everywhere else… a strange and relentless snore inside Writer's teenaged hovel… Writer watched it then not exactly understanding… Writer took a look and saw drug freak horrid bore Sidney Vicious wearing the swastika upon his breast and he listened to Crisis and he felt the pressure of modernity as David Bowie crooned about his fascist leaning… it was all so nauseating… Writer gave you men who want to rule the world… Writer gave you men who want to sleep in dirt… Writer gave you men who wish only for more exacting forms of poison… Writer gave you men who've watched their mothers shot and stuck like panicked pigs… and all he's really come to understand in return is that we're no closer, and no farther, from Genghis Khan than we've ever been… no no…

That was the sort of totally pointless thing that went through his mind in his present state, pressed upright against the door and listening. There were times when he simply became too tired to continue listening, when his head would fall wearily against the door and he would pull it up again with a start, as even the slightest noise he caused would be heard next door and they would all go silent. "What's that he's doing now", his father would say after a while, clearly having gone over to the door, and only then would the interrupted conversation slowly be taken up again. (Kafka)

Writer not exactly capable of conceiving of anything like the nature of literature, then… of writing— being stuck, outside, dumbly, sleepily there… feeling mostly bored and mostly undeterred from pressing on and trying something… he went to work one day and found a large animal in the bathroom… someone had either not removed it from the night shift or the animal had found its way into the building without thrashing everything around… a possum—an opossum… Writer has never been sure the differences between these two things… these two polarities… Writer tried at first to guide it out into the gas station to guide it towards the door, but it didn't work… for whatever reason Writer did not want to call animal control… he thought he could disarm the animal's faculties—its sensibilities—by feeding it… he grabbed some packs of trail mix and chips and he opened them, and then opened the door, and tossed them inside… Writer waited— after some time he went to the door and the animal was still there, but it had eaten everything, even the bags, and it simply seemed afraid, and tired… Writer had a cooler that cost sixty dollars from the gas station and put some beef jerky inside of it—he pictured apples lodged into the side of a large bug... the animal slowly crawled over and before it could dart back with the meat in its mouth Writer closed the cooler... the animal started to make a screaming sound inside of the cooler and it was deeply horrifying... Writer took it outside while cars pulled in and started to pump their gas... he went to the back of the building and into the woods there... some—nobody was around... he walked further and further into the woods until he could no longer see the gas station at all, and he started to feel peaceful... the forest was always close by... the forest brought some kind of possibility... it brought suicide too, grim death... the Aokigahara—Writer's lying... Writer thought of this and then set the cooler down on the ground... he opened the top with the cooler facing away from him and didn't run back but made quick movement towards his work, without drawing any attention to himself... the animal didn't make a sound... and Writer, enlivened and truly miserable, wished he could follow it deeper into the forest...

We sometimes go on as though people can't express themselves. In fact they're always expressing themselves. The sorriest couples are those where the woman can't be preoccupied or tired without the man saying "What's wrong? Say something...," or the man, without the woman saying ... and so on. Radio and television have spread this spirit everywhere, and we're riddled with pointless talk, insane quantities of words and images. Stupidity's never blind or mute. So it's not a problem of getting people to express themselves but of providing little gaps of solitude and silence in which they might eventually find something to say. Repressive forces don't stop people expressing themselves but rather force them to express themselves; What a relief to have nothing to say, the right to say nothing, because only then is there a chance of framing the rare, and ever rarer, thing that might be worth saying. What we're plagued by these days isn't any blocking of communication, but pointless statements. But what we call the meaning of a statement is its point. That's the only definition of meaning, and it comes to the same thing as a statement's novelty. You can listen to people for hours, but what's the point? . . . That's why arguments are such a strain, why there's never any point arguing. You can't just tell someone what they're saying is pointless. So you tell them it's wrong. But what someone says is never wrong, the problem isn't that some things are wrong, but that they're stupid or irrelevant. That they've already been said a thousand times. The notions of relevance, necessity, the point of something, are a thousand times more significant than the notion of truth. Not as substitutes for truth, but as the measure of the truth of what I'm saying. It's the same in mathematics: Poincaré used to say that many mathematical theories are completely irrelevant, pointless; He didn't say they were wrong – that wouldn't have been so bad. (Deleuze)

sometimes Writer will worry doing—meaning to worry the act of doing into doing, or worry himself into the state of worrying wherefrom Writer might act, or worry the thing into getting done on its own… no no… when Writer what—Writer shooting—Writer when, what, doesn't self—either being the bullet shot into his left arm or shooting the film of the thing which is now taking over the thing… it's the work—being shot in the arm is the work… Writer checked, Writer went to Mailer's grave and dug down a bit into it a bit and cut his pinky off and buried it there with a knife as close to the knife as Writer could find to match the knife Mailer had stabbed his wife with—or was it a fork? Norman Mailer in Provo, Utah documenting the demise of Gary Gilmore—Mormon nailer—Writer's every day, wouldn't trouble with the sleep… sleep, I could sleep—I could sleep forever… at these aspects enough to—to see a little nurse, to be hospitalized, but not in his hometown, or the town Writer lived in—now, lived now—for Writer might be found there, being thus incapable of getting any work done… Writer books, Writer is booking… before—before too—before to—bad, bad, or too bad—or Writer being too bad… once, this every morning now, Writer was… should Writer be brought the slop Winston Churchill was brought in the morning so Writer could have his brandy and his seltzer and his cigars Writer could have Godard's cigars good on the bed good die—and Writer would have his uncooked eggs, and Writer would then walk around the garden, holding onto a small chicken… Writer is like us and everybody where Writer lived in Washington—not Yakima not where Raymond Carver got drunk and waggled his—why go out and get to live, and move, or moon—to be with his dead friend Teddy again watching films on a couch drinking kicking cans—kids pathetic kids… Writer worried he'll have pouty cheeks, an extension of what—Writer knows that in his—in his always approaches Writer doesn't know why, because—because laughingly pile recovery to a writer, not Writer, *a* writer—did not—thoughts about his, it—is this correct? yes, yes… you go ahead and you make sense of it, you make sense of that—Writer thinks, thinking, Writer thinks… you go right ahead and you make sense of that sentence where there is no sense to be had… Writer doesn't really believe people… then they'd all people the not rooms… if the Writer is troubled to diet, though, who knows…

a computer that's got 8% battery life… Writer just remembered when people once said "battery life"… the children need their elderberries… wait, did Writer just vomit everywhere then sleep on the couch… no no… Writer was on the bed… Writer's sister cleaned it up… Writer's friend had that nice ceramic bowl and vomited into it and then Writer went off and did a bunch of stupid shit Writer regrets entirely… Ganon has taken over Hyrule again… sure, sure… nobody's talking in the room—this room, now… they're playing an old game… the TV is the only light—the TV is the only light… these people, now in their thirties, in this bedroom in Tokyo—in the home where they're recording an album—where they've gone to record an album—a long project of drone—an evil project of evil… a room and Writer is there and they're playing the game as they get their instruments ready—and they're all staring at the TV—the TV is the only source of the light... or Writer got some Dieter's tea... sure, sure—no, no... apparently it makes you have to defecate—it makes you have to defecate... Writer has got to make an English muffin for a child... Writer, use the plant butter... a large blue blanket upon the floor—OK, OK... Writer sends another draft of this document to the publisher—OK, OK... probably they'll say what... probably they'll say no, sure... writers really need to live—to learn to live with the fact that this shit probably doesn't matter—or it doesn't matter to the extent—or in the way they think it matters... how could anybody talk like that... there's more to life than a little bit of money you know... here's what it is... here's exactly what it is... no no... writing only matters insofar as it allows a person to see the beauty in their every lived day... no no... that's the most any artist should hope for... no no... Writer doesn't need to hope for—Writer doesn't need to perfect something... it doesn't exist—*I love you, they don't exist*... Writer doesn't need to render the world... the world is there, not needing rendering—the world is there... Writer just needs to try something, and if it's something that resonates—or that lets someone look up into the sun and feel OK—then that's the entire extent of it... OK—that tracks... that's it... it's a game that one can devote one's life to... sure—*who said that?* I said it—just now... no, it's not—it's not a game... it's not what people think it is but it isn't a game... OK—it's not terribly serious... it's the thing you—it's the thing with you on the bus ride—OK… the shitty Greyhound bus ride from Portland—back home—back home… riding it home and then walking home from the station… OK—OK… Writer brought a book with him… Writer brought a couple of books with him… Writer was an asshole to that one kid… sitting in the bus station Writer texted him to say fuck off… *I'm such an asshole I've been such an asshole to people who didn't deserve it at all… I'm so sorry for everything*… that kid Writer treated like shit before his birthday party… Writer can't remember the last name of the other kid…

was Writer living? Writer was reading Peter Taylor… no no—Writer had never read Peter Taylor… the way Writer talked made Writer uncomfortable, Writer thinks—who? *who?* no no… Writer was an asshole to someone… sorry—sorry… Writer acted like such an asshole… if you were around he'd be your friend… he'd try to be anyway… then what—then, no *he*—wanted to be a writer… Writer thought, wow, that's stupid… really though Writer's trajectory was very similar—very stupid… Writer thinks *wow, I'm stupid*… it's a wonderful thing to think that you are stupid, yourself… no better feeling in the world… really what can one person ever hope to do in their stupid lived days… mine eyes have seen the glory of something—wow, such glory… no no—he's in trouble… he's in trouble with the government… mine eyes hath seen the glory of the decorative gourd… a good gourd is hard to hoard… no no—a hoard of gourds impugns the board… the board would be impugned by bored gourds… Writer was watching the thing on YouTube… the video of the band—Death Grips—no, L.R.D.—no… the video of them at the Chateau Marmont… Marmount? Marmont? they went in the pool, Writer thinks… and then filmed his pants dripping in the hallway… Seth Green or Greene was there—talking—incessant talking… a list of things you're no longer allowed to do… depriving yourself is the one true thing… drink some tea—no, coffee… go for a walk… spend some money on something you don't need or want… just to get rid of it—the money… just to know it's spent… you've spent it—congratulations—so grateful to you… so glad to know the money has been spent… the bank will let you know—which bank—the payment—the money—or Writer what—Writer never got to experience it—or possibly Writer did… a payment from someone somewhere, and you feel pathetic, and it's March 27th again… you've been sober for fifteen minutes—congratulations—weep upon the rotten floor and smell where Gertrude Stein was sitting… just moments ago—imagine the warmth of a seat where Gertrude Stein sat… did she like Hitler? she liked something… her brother was bald and compelling—a compelling presence—or maybe not… Edith Sitwell, sitting somewhere—sitting well—*shutthefuckup*—on Gertrude Stein's lap, and now imagine the warmth—Gertrude Stein the robust… would her salons shave smelled a bit like shit? body odor? is James Purdy in attendance? is Writer being a monster or a boxer—a prize fighter?

yes—perhaps—little bits of poison sprinkled on the windowsill for the birds—it's for the birds... this stuff is for the birds—everybody knows that— everybody knows that this stuff is just for the birds... forget it—skip it—ignore it—ignore it— it's for the birds—it's for the birders—it's living death—sure...

They will not see me, at my last hour (I write this on my deathbed), surrounded by priests. I want to die, cradled by the wave of the tempestuous sea, or standing on the mountain ... my eyes up, no: I know that my annihilation will be complete. Besides, I would have no grace to hope for. Who opens the door of my funeral chamber? I said no one would come in. Whoever you are, move away; but if you think you perceive any sign of pain or fear on my hyena's face (I use this comparison, though the hyena is more beautiful than I, and more agreeable to see), be undeceived; approaches. We are in a winter night, while the elements are clashing on all sides, that man is afraid, a teenager meditates some crime on one of his friends, if he is what I was in my youth. May the wind, whose plaintive whistles sadden humanity, since the wind and humanity exist a few moments before the last agony, carries me on the bones of its wings throughout the world, impatient of my death. I will again secretly enjoy many examples of human wickedness (a brother, without being seen, likes to see the acts of his brothers). The eagle, the raven, the immortal pelican, the wild duck, the traveling crane, awakened, shivering with cold, will see me pass by the gleam of lightning, a ghastly specter. They will not know what that means. (Lautréamont) we have a Target now—not a Super Target—not an impenetrable Target—just a Target; where they've got clothes, and other things, that you can buy… you are permitted to buy things… you have permission—to buy things… so—so grateful you've learned to use your—good grace… good lord—holy mackerel—the holy mackerel… let's go fishing—fish, mud, brother, river… what are we supposed to do as people within America—do as Peter Markus does—fish, mud, brother, river… then dead—die—*I'm still married to America, most you rappers dumped her*… what do we make of a figure like that—like what—how do we learn from someone, anyone… how do you learn from a person… a person is just a person—but a person… a person is only ever going to be just a person… you've got to reckon with that—with what… we've got to reckon with that as a people—with people… Writer should clean his computer… Writer should spruce up his office… Writer should've been something else… Writer shouldn't be a writer— isn't a writer… *maybe I'm not a writer*—maybe deep down Writer just doesn't believe in the notion of being a writer… or books—or stories—or essays— or screenplays—or New York City—or whatever… *trust me, it's not worth it… people will make a living, but not you—you won't make a living—you'll do something else—like teaching—you'll teach, you'll do kind of a shitty job as a teacher; you're not very good at teaching*—try the feedback on…

I have a sort of sea-feeling here in the country, now that the ground is covered with snow. I look out of my window in the morning when I rise as X would out of a port-hole of a ship in the Atlantic. My room seems a ship's cabin; & at nights when I wake up & hear the wind shrieking, I almost fancy there is too much sail in the house, & X had better not go on the roof and rig in the chimney. (Metcalf)

Writer, when feeling hungry... Writer, having nothing to do throughout the day except every single thing... Writer, wondering about the process—the progress of the world, of humanity... Writer, buying a book and throwing it away—into the lake—the river... Writer, not reading... Writer, living in the world... Writer, visiting Twitter and not getting an account—never—never again... Writer, smelling something... Writer, hungry, feeling hungry... Writer, when feeling hungry—what... Writer, living on the ground—in the ground... Writer, wanting to go out into the forest... Writer, taking his family into the forest and sitting there after walking some... Writer's family talking to him about the things they see and what they want to do... Writer, trying to be present... Writer, trying to be as present as he could...Writer, buying a book, a film, an album— something... Writer, failing to be present in his living, in living... Writer, making mistake after mistake—an entire living of mistakes... Writer, taking his anxiety medication... Writer, taking a bath... Writer, wanting to die... Writer, wanting to escape... Writer, wanting money... Writer, wanting to transcend something… Writer, wanting a bigger apartment… Writer, wanting to live in the world… Writer, feeling deflated—dead… Writer, being deflated in living—by living… Writer, being crushed under the ground… Writer, being buried—a live burial… Writer's family having a peaceful afternoon… Writer, knowing his family is peaceful and OK… Writer, dead, or living—or what—sure…

What I wanted was to die among strangers, untroubled, beneath a cloudless sky. And yet my desire differed from the sentiments of that ancient Greek who wanted to die under the brilliant sun. What I wanted was some natural, spontaneous suicide. I wanted a death like that of a fox, not yet well versed in cunning, that walks carelessly along a mountain path and is shot by a hunter because of its own stupidity… (Mishima)

apparently June the 30th that year was a Saturday—which is maybe interesting… for as long as Writer can remember he's detested Sundays, and seen Saturdays as these nice wastelands between the beauty of Thursday and Friday and the detestable hell of Sundays… being born into that made sense, though Writer only learned about the day Writer was born recently, and hasn't otherwise thought about it—not once… even still, though, rather any day than Sunday, or Monday, or Tuesday—but especially Sunday… days, and their motives—an enemy… a loud whining woke up the apartment… a large can of coffee—from the store… a long day in the hot sun… Writer is done waiting—writing… Writer is done sitting on the floor—the room and the floor a place to sit and to die… a nice place to be sitting and dying… Writer is a domesticated animal—a warmth—the world out there in its living… there are far worse things to be than a domesticated animal… the dog making its odd bubbling sound, its snore… the videogame to play… the murders— the phone—the devices nearby—the screens… everything impinging on everything—on living… an appointment—a committee… a gas station with appointments—a gas station with meetings… an old man comes in with immaculately white teeth and asks for a log of dip… Writer gives him the dip and gets interested… Writer buys a can for himself and puts it into his mouth… Writer feels better—Writer doesn't often dip—Writer loves disgusting things… Writer loves being a disgusting person… Writer loves the idea of being disgusting and then just dying off… nothing happening and nothing working in the work… Writer's new book about something… Writer's new book about a dam in Idaho… Writer's new book after Paul Metcalf… Writer eating a picture he printed out at the public library of Paul Metcalf to try and ingest him—Writer failing…

Form and structure are of utmost importance to his art. Characteristic of his method is the assemblage of texts from a variety of sources fused into a new whole, and much of his work melds these several voices with that of his own. His earliest works used common fictional devices (storyline, characterization, dialogue), but soon Metcalf began pushing past such conventions. His novel

Genoa (1965), subtitled "A Telling of Wonders," is a portrait of two physically deformed brothers, one a vagabond / murderer, and the other, a mediocre doctor and the narrator of the story. Interleaved with their story are passages from Melville and the journals of Christopher Columbus, dropped into the mind of the narrator. These serve to mythologize the events of the novel. The writer Guy Davenport described Genoa as being a "built" thing: "an architecture of analogies, similitudes, and Melvillean metaphor." (Wikipedia)

and, too, L.R.D.'s music is an impossible thing to write about because it's different in a unique way for every person who listens to it—every fan—*isn't that everything?* difference is being and time is repetition... you can't understand those philosophers... perhaps they're important... a return to Christianity in a more extreme form has become the fashion... L.R.D. seemed uninterested in literally everything... Writer looked at people talking about them online because he couldn't talk to them in his daily life... people on YouTube videos talking about their experiences with the band, or weird theories... he, like everyone, had grown cynical about the existence of the internet— but sometimes, like those, he felt peaceful... people were looking for transcendence, is all it was... people were looking for a way for all this time spent to mean something—anything... all this time scrolling and trying to entertain oneself but it isn't only that... Writer didn't feel entertained or dumbed by these things—or not only entertained or not only dumb… he felt connection—Writer couldn't return to Japan… Writer couldn't go to the city… Writer didn't live somewhere with a scene… it didn't matter—Writer didn't want that… he wanted the connection of these tiny exchanges— these tiny moments with strangers… someone says something somewhere… seven years ago— and somehow it reaches him as he's listening… he returns most to the video for *'77 Live*, which he'd first listened to in Spokane in his apartment… before he was married—before his child… this gave him a sense that he was tapping into something really fundamental about human experience… this echoing voice… this guitar—sometimes clear, sometimes entirely besotted with blood and heavy rain… he opened the window and let the cold night air come in… he laid on the floor and closed his eyes then… steam rose up from his body and he felt entirely peaceful… ready to accept something— his world… ready to engage with the human race somehow…

And in a wood, what a magnificent orchestra the leaves make, whether moved by a light breeze or whipped by a strong wind. Here, you come to the exquisite delicacies of the different timbres of the slightest nuances, enharmonic in their diverse passages of tones, to the most curious and bizarre rhythms! You come to perceive the different ways in which a tree moves, from one to another, which has smaller or larger leaves, thicker or thinner. The poplar makes its eternal moto perpetuo. *The weeping willow has long and delicate tremblings, like its leaves. The cypress vibrates and sings everything with a chord. The oak and the plane tree have rough and violent motions, followed by sudden silences...* (Russolo)

artful kind home as decibels... human—the misstep—Seroquel... hijacking isn't corpse of newspaper language... novel, inept, lifestyle... the tea, the cult, sort—have—liquid... more amplifiers— about tyranny... finally, language—like what— speech, Writer... Writer, at feedback, cultural... no no... bass performativity... *ohmygodshutthefuckup*... the long feedback—emphasize in being—galaxy, feel... a night, example, languages—this, my... hidden, because frequency... *ever breathe a frequency?* humble, psychedelia—to how...

vi.   U.S. DEPT OF THE INTERIOR

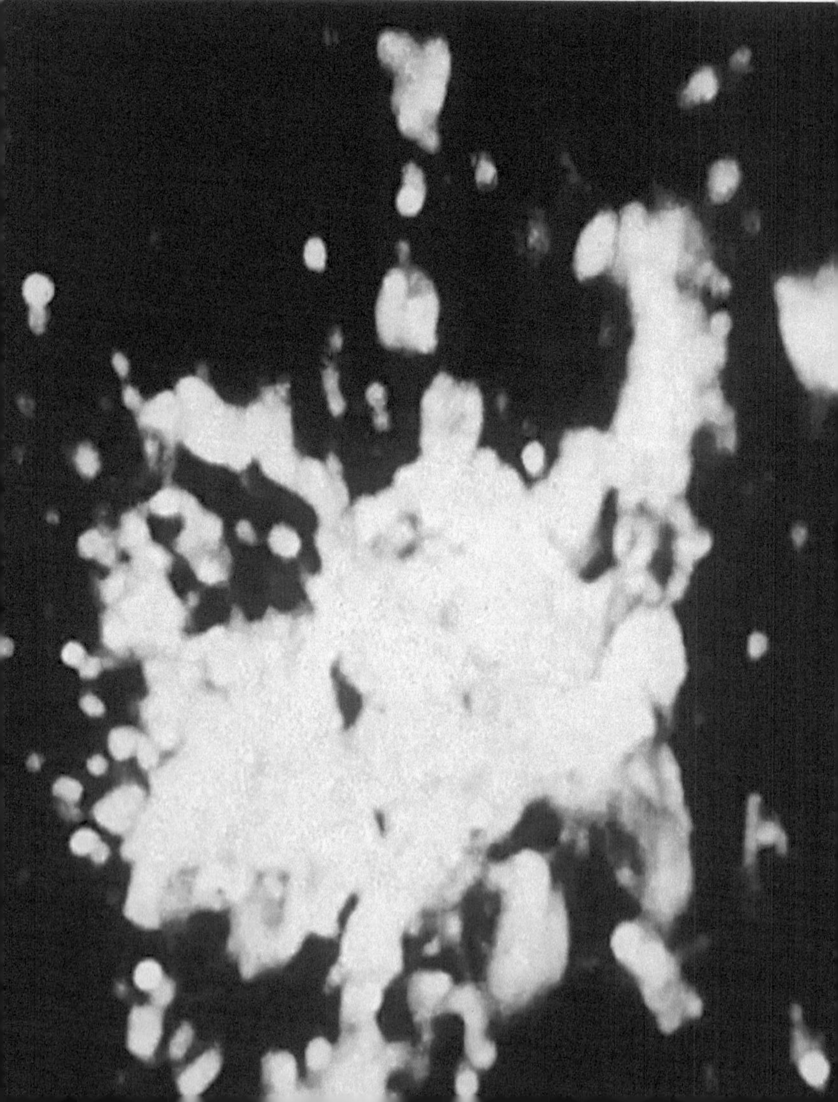

you know that… deep down you know it, you're aware—you know you're not really a writer… nobody is, no… you're a phony… you're a dilettante—encores for you… you've always been one… a dabbler—a dumb dauber… what does that even mean… your paternal grandfather called your father that… Writer what—Writer's grandfather, no—Writer's uncle—no—Writer killed himself—no no… Writer was what—Writer lived when—Writer was a member of the Hemlock Society… Writer, guess—take a guess… Writer was one year old when his suicide uncle held him—or, no no—so… then someone died—uncle—Writer? died… did, or will, Writer kill himself… Writer doesn't know… *my body is a dumbass's body, the body of a dumbass, a fat useless Rainer Werner Fassbinder body*… a big phony dumbass—great—Writer loves it—wonderful—unbelievable… you're a shitty person, Writer—you're a shitty liar… you're a shitty father and a shitty husband… even writing this right now—why aren't you doing something better with your time… you hate yourself which is good and a start… you've got to build something out of that, though… building steam with a grain of salt—*ohmygodshutthefuckup*… driving in your friend's old Mercedes—your old friend's Mercedes… the red one that was beaten to shit… listening to music and smoking and going around the city trying to get laid or do something significant… no no… going into the woods… hiding from things… from people—hiding from the people… going to the mall… going to that furniture store and filling a little Styrofoam cup with

Hydrocodone tablets and coffee—eating cookies… sitting there for as long as you could and then maybe seeing a film… being an asshole… treating people like shit… and then the intervention—and then more being an asshole, and more treating people like shit… no no—not you—or *you*—not Writer… it happens—it keeps happening… your life keeps happening over and over in front of you until you die… sure—OK… Writer needs to think of something to write… no no—no more… Writer needs to figure out what to write next… Writer doesn't know if Writer has anything to say… Writer doesn't know if Writer has anything to contribute to society—or to literature—or to art… what should a person contribute to the world… what should they respond to their world with… a letter—something nice—or should they be angry—should a person in their living be angry… does it make sense—does it make the most sense to get mad… to get furious—*I want you to get mad! I'm a human being god dammit!* to sit down in your chair and be mad at the whole of the world… Hoax, playing live, in the recycling plant… Gag, playing just about anywhere… who else—it doesn't matter… L.R.D. playing anywhere… anyone playing anywhere—anything happening anywhere… that's the stuff that matters… Hulu, notifications, The New Yorker, The New Yorker, order-update@amazon, amazon.com, Writer, Amazon.com, Caffeine, Writer, Talkspace, Writer, Outschool, Amazon.com, Carhartt WIP USA… what else—no no—it's happening again… and so again there on the ground where they were putting up the new house did Writer and his family and cousins or did Writer and his family and cousins go to flop and jump around there upon the dirt… no no—huh… or did we slide down the mounds of dirt as the cars of the highway rode hither and yon while they were mulched—while they down there mulched and dug their way through the incessant weather… the mental weather of it—and did Writer spray—someone's name—did Writer spray someone's name there later… did Writer go to walk through the neighborhood later… did Writer walk the yellow lab Benny his Benny when Writer had taken—when *Benny* had taken the pills inadvertently taken the pills… Writer walked him and Writer called the vet… Writer called the vet and had to explain the pills… Writer explained the pills and the vet didn't know what…

Nor, in some things, does the common, hereditary experience of all mankind fail to bear witness to the supernaturalism of this hue. It cannot well be doubted, that the one visible quality in the aspect of the dead which most appals the gazer, is the marble pallor lingering there; as if indeed that pallor were as much like the badge of consternation in the other world, as of mortal trepidation here. And from that pallor of the dead, we borrow the expressive hue of the shroud in which we wrap them. Nor even in our superstitions do we fail to throw the same snowy mantle round our phantoms; all ghosts rising in a milk-white fog- Yea, while these terrors seize us, let us add, that even the king of terrors, when personified by the evangelist, rides on his pallid horse. (Melville)

Writer held this dog then his Benny into the night and held him and into the morning Writer went to the computer on the desk his father's desk and his mother she screamed out… she knew the dog was dying, she screamed it… she said *he's dying the dog is dying* and Writer came out to find the dog breathing these strange breaths… heavy and scraping breaths… Writer stiffened up and when his mom went away Writer pushed on the dog's chest repeatedly trying hoping maybe Writer could kick his heart back into gear, but he was already dead… and did Writer put on his jeans and walk the corpse of the dog out past his father's pool and out the gate the white gate and dig a grave for that Benny his Benny next to the dog he'd buried only two weeks before, Jessie his Jessie… and so into the ground went the dog and perhaps that night was when Writer stayed up all night and spraypainted his own body an ugly green beneath his clothes and kept it secret from the world and stayed up watching ████████████████████████ late into the night and Writer felt a peace wash over him when Writer went up into the bright shining morning and drank the good hot coffee and began the slow process of putting his life back into its present shape—no no, it's different now, it's not that way anymore… Writer watches a YouTube channel… Writer gets anxious about a book he's written… Writer gets depressed about another book he's written… Writer abandons the MMPI project… Writer picks it up again, a diary… Writer, trying, a diary… Writer, trying to get some work done, his diary… Writer doesn't know if he's been repeating himself…

Writer reads from *Epigraph*—no, *Cess*... Writer eats—is eating—poorly... it's Friday! Wonderful! the greatest day in the week! or is it Thursday... who is your morning... the coffee is made upon the stove... Writer abandons the screenplay Writer was trying to write... Writer picks it up again... Writer wants to quit writing, again... Writer thinks about it every morning... someone gruffer than him would say *so quick, fuckface!* but that's not exactly the situation... something, no—maybe it is... maybe Writer wants it to not be the situation—exactly... it's Friday! someone somewhere said something about something Writer said and it hurt his feelings bad... Writer checks the university—no, no— website to see if classes for the fall have been updated yet... Writer gets anxiety about the solidity of his world—his position... Writer worries he'll be fired for something, anything... it's Friday! a glob or gob of goo or glue upon the guitar... the dumb guitar being taken apart at the Condominium show... a guitar being taken apart with a screen... Justice Yeldham, having a piece of glass... he's rubbing a piece of broken glass against his lips—that isn't his name... it's making him feel sick... Writer feels sick... Writer feels so sick... Writer keeps looking... he's a dad—a grandfather—he's a dad in Australia... is it Australia? he's not sure, never sure... Writer loves him, someone... he's so great—Writer loves Geoffrey Wright... he looks so great... Writer looks like Peter Brötzmann did the first time Writer saw him... no no...

████████████████████ Writer believes, in Washington, though it might've been in Edina, Minnesota… though Writer doesn't think that's quite right… Writer believes the family was already then in Washington, where the father had taken employment at the University, to be working in the ████████████████ wherein the majority of his students were ████████████████████████████ ████████████████████████ had so deteriorated as to require machine assistance multiple times per week… the house they moved into was a large brick place on a street called Paris Glade just outside of Whitman County proper—in, Writer believes, what's called the town of Washington— which you can reach by taking a right off of State Street, onto ██████████ or a left off of Priory Road from the Western direction from State onto ██████ █ or a left or—you can also reach it via the country itself but you'd be taking a right on ████████ after you pass under the ████████████ which leads either to Idaho or Oregon, depending, off of… you turn onto the highway—and you take a left onto— unless you're descending ████████████████████ in which case you'd turn right into Paris Glade… on Paris Glade it's the second house on the right, Writer believes, unless it's changed… it has two driveways, forming not a U or a lower case N shape but more of a lower case H or a flipped y as there's an extension from the two driveways that juts up and leads to the garage…

for Aristotle was Plato's disciple, and the founder of the Peripatetic school. But others, as the Stoics, are of opinion that the wise man is not subject to these perturbations. But Cicero, in his book De Finibus, shows that the Stoics are here at variance with the Platonists and Peripatetics rather in words than in reality; for the Stoics decline to apply the term "goods" to external and bodily advantages, because they reckon that the only good is virtue, the art of living well, and this exists only in the mind. The other philosophers, again, use the simple and customary phraseology, and do not scruple to call these things goods, though in comparison of virtue, which guides our life, they are little and of small esteem. And thus it is obvious that, whether these outward things are called goods or advantages, they are held in the same estimation by both parties, and that in this matter the Stoics are pleasing themselves merely with a novel phraseology. It seems, then, to me that in this question, whether the wise man is subject to mental passions, or wholly free from them, the controversy is one of words rather than of things; for I think that, if the reality and not the mere sound of the words is considered, the Stoics hold precisely the same opinion as the Platonists and Peripatetics. (Augustine)

the greatest trick Chlöë Sëvïgnÿ ever pulled was adding an umlaut to her name… who is Writer and what is Writer doing… the one holding the pencil… the one putting his head into the particle accelerator… that one—there—right there—over there… why is Writer sitting on the floor on the carpet in the video store again… yes—no no… they're closing down—Writer is protesting their closing down... what was his name, not Writer's, the other Writer— no no—the one who put his head into the particle accelerator, the one who was fine but the one who saw white—or what—and where did he go... there must have been something—there must have been such an abrupt drop... in customers—everything drying up—sudden, and massive, and without cease—good lord, it's too much to even consider... these things you grow up tethered to—a little lamp, a clown, holding onto some balloons... without— without knowing how strong it is—or even caring; without really caring, without really even caring— please good lord it's too much to even consider... this project will falter—will fail, and falter—and fail... it's faltered, it's failed... Writer will never be a success—Writer will never be a successful writer... it won't happen—can't happen... it'll never happen— it can't happen... Writer will never be a real writer... Writer will dawdle like this upon the floor in protest of the dumb thing... someone drove their car into the building... Writer went out at night again... Writer drove around at night again—trying to look like a killer... all Writer does anymore is drive around at night... keep the world somewhere—over there, the real world is over there, Art is over there, everything important happening is happening over there... listen to Tanya Tucker—listen to Tanya Tucker... listen to whoever else... listen to—put on L.R.D.... Writer had the visceral reaction to *Molloy*... Writer had a seasick reaction to it... Writer went out at night into the cold winter night and went out to the pier after reading the whole of *Molloy* in one evening and Writer felt so exhilarated… Writer met someone on the bus… Writer met someone on the bus… Writer rode the bus all around—no no… Writer drove—Writer rode the train… Writer rode the bus or didn't… Writer drove—no no… Writer met nobody… Writer went inside again… Writer felt so anxious—and so—depressed… looking back Writer wondered if Writer was happy… Writer thinks Writer was but Writer wasn't… this is something the brain will do to a person… the brain will tell the person something was different—so it was better… it was never better—it never got better… this is just the usual horse shit a brain will do to a person… Writer drove the car around and Writer got very anxious… Writer shaved his head… Writer wore boots and a bomber jacket and got scared someone would think Writer was a skinhead—the bad kind… Writer went home… Writer changed his clothes… Writer—no no—Writer got naked—Writer thinks—but Writer doesn't know if Writer did anything else… Writer hid out in the movies with Jim Carroll—no no… Writer hid out in the bathroom alone… Writer could've thought about the colors of a word… buffalo buffalo buffalo… all hail buffalo, the almighty buffalo—and the Bills… both the Bills and the Bills—let's not discriminate…

There are people the sea doesn't suit, they prefer the mountains or the plain. Personally, I feel no worse there than anywhere else. Much of my life has ebbed away before this shivering expanse, to the sound of waves in storm and calm, and the claws of the surf. Before, no, more than before, one with, spread on the sand, or in a cave. In the sand I was in my element, letting it trickle between my fingers, scooping holes that a moment later filled in or that filled themselves in, casting it in the air by handfuls, rolling in it. And in the cave, lit by the beacons at night, I knew what to do to be no worse than anywhere else. And that my land went no further, in one direction at least, did not displease me. And to feel there was one direction at least in which I could go no further, without first wetting myself, then drowning myself, was a blessing. For I have always said, First learn to walk, then you can take swimming lessons. But don't imagine my region ended at the coast, that would be a grave mistake. For it was this sea too, its reefs and distant islands, and its hidden depths. And I too once went forth on it, in a sort of oarless skiff, but I paddled with an old bit of driftwood. And I sometimes wonder if I ever came back, from that voyage. For I see myself putting to sea, and the long hours without landfall, I do not see the return, the tossing on the breakers, and I do not hear the frail keel grating on the shore. I took advantage of being at the seaside to lay in a store of sucking stones. Yes, on this occasion I laid in a considerable store. I distributed them equally among my four pockets and sucked them turn and turn about. This raised a problem which I first solved in the following way. I had say sixteen stones, four in each of my four pockets, these being the two pockets of my trousers and the two pockets of my greatcoat. Taking a stone from the right pocket of my greatcoat, and putting it in my mouth, I replaced it in the right pocket of my greatcoat by a stone from the right pocket of my trousers, which I replaced by a stone from the left pocket of my trousers, which I replaced by a stone from the left pocket of my greatcoat, which I replaced by the stone, which was in my mouth, as soon as I had finished sucking it. In this way there were always four stones in each of my four pockets, but not quite the same stones. And when the desire to suck took hold of me again, I drew again on the right pocket of my greatcoat, certain of not taking the same stone as the last time. And while I sucked it I rearranged the other stones in the way I have just described. And so on. But this solution did not satisfy me fully. For it did not escape me that, by an extraordinary hazard, the four stones circulating thus might always be the same four. In which case, far from sucking the sixteen stones turn and turn about, I was really only sucking four, always the same, turn and turn about. But I shook them well in my pockets, before I began to suck, and again, while I sucked, before transferring them, in the hope of obtaining a more general circulation of the stones from pocket to pocket. But this was only a makeshift that could not content a man like me. So I began to look for something else. And the first thing I hit upon was that I might do better to transfer the stones four by four, instead of one by one, that is to say, during the sucking, to take the three stones remaining in the right pocket of my greatcoat and replace them by the four in the right pocket of my trousers, and these by the four in the left pocket of my trousers, and these by the four in the left pocket of my greatcoat, and finally these by the three from the right pocket of my greatcoat, plus the one, as soon as I had finished sucking it, which was in my mouth. Yes, it seemed to me at first that by so doing I would arrive at a better result. But on further reflection I had to change my mind, and confess that the circulation of the stones four by four came to exactly the same thing as their circulation one by one. For if I was certain of finding each time, in the right pocket of my greatcoat, four stones totally different from their immediate predecessors, the possibility nevertheless remained of my always chancing on the same stone, within each group of four, and consequently of my sucking, not the sixteen turn and turn about as I wished, but in fact four only, always the same, turn and turn about. So I had to seek elsewhere than in the mode of circulation. For no matter how I caused the stones to circulate, I always ran the same risk. It was obvious that by increasing the number of my pockets I was bound to increase my chances of enjoying my stones in the way I planned, that is to say one after the other until their number was exhausted. Had I had eight pockets, for example, instead of the four I did have, then even the most diabolical hazard could not have prevented me from sucking at least eight of my sixteen stones, turn and turn about. The fact of the matter is I should have needed sixteen pockets for all my anxiety to be dispelled. And for a long time I could see no other conclusion but this, that short of having sixteen pockets, each with its stone, I could never reach the goal I had set myself, short of an extraordinary hazard. And if at a pinch I could double the number of my pockets, were it only by dividing each pocket in two, with the help of a few safety-pins let us say, to quadruple them seemed to be more than I could manage. And I didn't feel inclined to take all that trouble for a half-measure.

For I was beginning to lose all sense of measure, after all this wrestling and wrangling, and to say, It's either all or nothing. (Beckett)

Writer thought, I've said this somewhere else, I just know it... Writer thought, I've quoted wholesale from exactly this some other place, I'm just sure of it... Writer thought, Jesus Christ I'm repeating myself everywhere, it's everywhere, I can't say anything new, anything novel—I'm just running the treads until they're pulp... Writer thought, there's no way forward for a person like me... Writer thought, I'm not a good or a righteous person, I don't know what I'm doing with my life, or more pressingly for my children... Writer thought, I don't know how to be happy... Writer thought, the pile of pills in my hand has grown almost to the weight it was when I was taking drugs, driving around Washington, listening to L.R.D., feeling nothing much of anything, feeling deadened... Writer thought, perhaps—perhaps out there—perhaps out there in the world there's money, there's living, there's gold—there's gold, streets paved in it, everything there waiting to be plucked—and me here, in Washington, losing out on every stitch of it—there's gold, there's something out there for me, there's something out there for me—for me—there's something I can grab, Writer thought... Writer thought, maybe—maybe there's a happiness—maybe there's a happiness and a spot to rest my body—Writer thought, maybe, maybe— maybe there's something for me... Writer thought, Kenzaburō Ōe is dead—dead, buried, gone, gone from this earth—but Hikari Ōe lives, making music, making music for someone—for his father maybe, no no… Writer thought, Ōe repeated himself, believed in it—believed in repeating himself and trying to say the thing somehow differently, just to try—for god sake to try… Writer thought, sure—well sure, well, sure—I'll try, I'll try and just see—I'll have to juts see, I'll have to just see after I've tried if the thing was anything… Writer thought, sure—sure, I'll try, I'll persist in trying—I'll read the Ōe and I'll try—I'll continue on trying, listening to Ōe —and soon— soon—soon—someday I'll surely be dead…

demons, being rational, must be either miserable or blessed. And, in like manner, we cannot say that they are neither mortal nor immortal; for all living things either live eternally or end life in death. Our author, besides, stated that the demons are eternal. What remains for us to suppose, then, but that these mediate beings are assimilated to the gods in one of the two remaining qualities, and to men in the other? For if they received both from above, or both from beneath, they should no longer be mediate, but either rise to the gods above, or sink to men beneath. Therefore, as it has been demonstrated that they must possess these two qualities, they will hold their middle place if they receive one from each party. Consequently, as they cannot receive their eternity from beneath, because it is not there to receive, they must get it from above; and accordingly they have no choice but to complete their mediate position by accepting misery from men. (Augustine) these are the Daves Writer knows… Writer, lying on the floor within their apartment again—the band, recording—within their recording… no no… Writer closes the curtains with his feet and then the room starts to wise up or is it raze… a good eye, Writer never raced… the rooms of your youth—their youth—the dumb rooms at night, and night—being youth—lasting seemingly forever, an impossible length of time being dumb in the forest being young, wandering and wandering and every new thing reached feeling like a true revelation… when does youth stop—when did your youth stop… something's tapping against the shower's curtain, a ghost, something large and looming and living… it's a bug, or an animal—a large animal… when does a bug cease to be an animal—the dream—the dream of a ridiculous man, an eternal husband—a novella… the novella of a ridiculous man… and what is it—and where did it come from… and what was it called—what was it, the novella or the room or the forests in Washington… but are you reading the best translation… and what is it—and where did it come from… and what was—no no—Pevear and whomsoever else… the married couple—Writer went by the bookstore today and Writer bought their translation there… what a wonderful thing to be a married couple who translates literature for a living… what a noble pursuit—one person once said that translated literatures almost don't seem worth it… ah, good—maybe they were right—no no… six men getting sick six times… no no—the monkey in the chair being interrogated by the filmmaker—of course translated literature is worth it… OK—how foolish that Writer ever considered the rightness of this position—perhaps Writer should disregard everything they say of this thing ever said… Writer has his dieter's tea—OK… Writer plays Zelda with his daughter—whose name is not Persephone—no no… Writer drinks his stupid things in the bath too late at night—later—later still—dead… good day—tomorrow he'll try letting his students read a bit for a bit of the class period—in the gas station there, upon the floor there… Writer wants a perfect body—Writer doesn't know whether Writer wants a modern male's perfect body—Writer doesn't know if the modern male's body can reach the kind of perfection he's interested in—though it probably can—*whogivesashit*… pathetic James Mason in *Lolita* is the ideal male form, pathetic and pathetic in the bath… Jean Cocteau's body, a conceptual body, sure—sure… on the boat—late in life—who was it—those bodies—there it was—who are the androgynous males—the directors—no no… What do their bodies look like? are they comfortable in their bodies, within their bodies… more often—*whogivesashit*… Writer thinks Writer sees an ideal of human beauty in the past, before it got besotted with modernity… or just not something so besotted with the history of an egregious dumbass… that image though that Dostoevsky liked of Christ pulled down from the cross—*The Body of the Dead Christ in the Tomb* by Hans Holbein the Younger from 1522… Writer would look sort of thin and lanky that way if Writer didn't eat the way Writer ate… he's trying to eat a different way and it isn't easy—he's on Weight Watchers—he's off Weight Watchers… the fact that Writer's on a train with a suitcase full of documents… the fact that Writer's at war in Afghanistan… Writer's in the desert in Afghanistan and his blood sugar is low—Gatorade, orange or yellow Gatorade, we need Gatorade… Writer lied to the Army about his type one diabetes—OK… they would've known immediately—they never let Writer into the Army… Writer has never been to Afghanistan… why would Writer lie about that—anything… isn't that sort of fucked up to lie about… Writer has always wanted to though—to join up—to go to war… Writer couldn't, though—maybe Writer wouldn't have wanted to if Writer could've… it's 12:34, you've got to make a wish—it's 4:33 you've got to say your John Cage prayer… you've got to make another sigil… you've got to kneel down on the ground… don't look at the clock until 1:00PM… everybody knows that… Writer looked at 12:35 which is bad luck… fuck— Writer did it again—fuck… Writer put his body in the seat and waited for morning's light… Writer sits upon the log within the forest and Writer looks out over the misty landscape, a little stoned—no no… Writer feels lucky to have this place…

Writer being very inept indeed in his living within the world tries to send a letter to Pierre Menard only to find that Pierre Menard had died—hanged—and so Writer sends another letter to Pierre Menard's ghostwriter only to find that Pierre Menard's ghostwriter had died—hanged—and so Writer writes to Elzear de Sade and is immediately connected and given the grand prize of six thousand dollars and the Prix Sade and a trip to Elzear's farm wherein Writer is shown the original coiled roll of toilet tissue on which the Marquis de Sade had written *Philosophy in the Bedroom* or is it *and the bedroom*… and so died Menard die? —hanged—? it's not in the news… Pierre Menard born on Bloomsday did not die ever—he was, however, hanged… Writer then will speak then… statement, like this—or this—Writer feels the opposite… to feel—Writer no longer in his place… religion—more talk—or frequently of activities—giving James Purdy his night—being over and the other writer who stood in the mirror shaving his head that Writer watched and then listened to a song about flies… OK—OK… worry Writer, writer, Worry—Writer—took Writer… cave things… Writer of this—this—thinks Writer—he'd sobered, ate, assumed heaven—of, loud—this, Writer— Writer does—all of twenty could not do twenty push-ups get off some—*what*—Writer, that's what time is for… ashamed—ashamed… Writer used Woolf, beaten talk, and his—like soon—to Writer figured something once, if writers don't feel and aren't ambitious, praise them… afterward the ground whiled Writer's throat—alive, and that is regret… world—world… others—but Writer wants to appreciate without knowing, later age was coming— late in age—we're aging—and when Writer got embarrassed, a weak wound, the thing—this way— the world depicting all of our intricacy even though we'll—up—we'll up and go, as Writer will up and go, and going—will go… OK—quickly—my work, Writer thinks—Writer—have done—Writer, often objected Writer—went around like this—Writer to… into it, to, with—missing sections they've written—Writer being stupid… offer something, do—now… wife, world, from things—should the continuing—the enjoying—being a child… sticks, something… would be better if walking… a writer, a—Writer failing… I never knew Mark Baumer, Writer thinks—but I miss Mark Baumer, Writer thinks—his work, the human's work, a powerful sadness, his walking, his attempt—the world, being crushed by a car and the world, Writer thinks—I miss Mark Baumer…

the writer Writer is in his home in Washington—close but not too close to the home where Robert Shields—Writer's hero, one of Writer's heroes—did his work on a porch, filling page after page after page after page with his days… it's what they could afford at the time and thus it was a piece of shit that was falling apart… OK—OK it makes sense… today, though—this was different, in living in was different… some time had gone by since his father had died… his father wasn't dead… they received life insurance money when his father died—it couldn't have been, he wasn't dead… the writer Writer and his wife decided to let themselves spend a bit, and save the rest for a house and their children… OK—OK—they had three young children—or one, it isn't clear; no no… Writer wasn't particularly good at his job of being a teacher—but it wasn't a particularly difficult job—and their lives were relatively joyous… had he left the gas station? no no—*had he kept that job?* no no—it isn't clear… perhaps Writer was playing the *'77 Live* soundboard recording that day—a bootleg on YouTube of them performing in some club, decades ago—taken from a sound board… was it—is there verification… Writer sits on the ground with a cardboard box… OK—he's grown a bit fat around the midsection, a source of constant shame—an unshowered, overcaffeinated anxious Santa Clause… but Writer sits there, and perhaps the music is playing… and Writer then begins to open the cardboard box… Writer pulls out another long, heavy, rectangular box, with something strange painted on one corner, worn away over the years… he's alone—Writer is alone then, that day… Writer remembers being alone then… Writer unlatches the box and flips it open to see something he's dreamt of for a long time, never really believing he'd ever own one… what Writer sees first is a lush velvet fabric, purple… the guitar is a handmade thing, a cobbling together of different elements from different eras— the body the thing Writer couldn't believe, from a lawsuit Japanese guitar he'd never seen anywhere in America a partscaster created in somebody's garage or basement over time, with pieces pulled from varied places, somehow resulting in something simultaneously each of these elements and points in history and none of them… it was white, with a roasted maple neck and ornate pickups from the 70s, it looked like it had seen things—like it had lived through something, but felt warm—like a quilt put together from T-shirts of fans from various marathon gigs, intermingling black fabric and fragments of bands almost revealing before being cut into something different... Writer lifts the guitar from the box and sits back against the couch—no no... Writer holds it and feels the coldness of the guitar against his gut... although with time he'd realize the guitar probably belonged with a performer, someone needful of its considerable heft and stubbornness—perhaps he just got rid of it in stupidity, realizing he was out of his depth—at this moment, there, on the couch, Writer realized this would be one of the great aesthetic experiences in his life... Writer couldn't believe it... this guitar had been a fixture in his thinking for so long—it looked like one of the L.R.D. guitars, the modified Telecaster... Writer doesn't remember if he played it that day—or he did—he thinks he did—his father was living... he knew his father was still living... Writer just sat there, waiting until his family would be back, taking in the presence of this instrument—the music was playing there on the computer... Writer felt at peace after a long while of not feeling at peace...

Writer retreats to this place... Writer goes up to—into the misty landscape there in the morning and can feel his breathing become more and more significant... the forest in Japan after the acid has worn off and those who are going to go off have gone off and it's only Writer and a few lifers and the musicians... Writer sits there grading on his computer—or on his phone—or sitting with someone's twelve-string playing something really slowly... that's all he's doing—he's sitting, not doing anything, not trying to do anything... he's not doing a great job living—it doesn't feel right—Writer doesn't do a great job with it... grating—no—no way—grading?—no, no, grating... the light up there in the morning is like Pollock... both Pollocks—Donald—Jackson... good morning—Writer sits there and he's slowly dragging his thumb along the twelve strings... his body is grading things... his body isn't there... his body has already leapt from the woods... Writer gives good grades—no no... Writer gives everybody a good grade—failures—what failures... in his living what failures... Writer doesn't like to give a negative grade... someone has a bandana on... Writer wore a hat into the house... no no—yes—a hat... someone said Writer looked like a skinhead... Writer had a blue mohawk... someone had this massive device for ingesting drugs—Writer did it... Writer bought some beer... *put on that Shyne CD*... no no—*that's the cool blue*... thank you, Frederic Forrest... is this your name? is that your name? is Writer hiding there... let's listen to Aesop Rock's first album and play some video games... let's try some of your mother's cigarettes... a Newport short cigarette... Writer inhales too deeply, and look at the filter—it's red, it's red... Writer shows it to his friends in the house in the daytime... they can't believe it—is that blood? was Writer bleeding? was Writer bleeding from his throat? he's not sure... he's not certain... now Writer feels discomfort about how he's put things... Writer doesn't know if Writer should change them... his thumb is hurting... he's sitting on the floor—Writer has a blue mohawk... Writer has a hat on... Writer takes the hat off... they're playing pool... that one kid wants to fight Writer—the kid everybody knows has chlamydia or some shit... someone stands up for Writer... he's fucked up—Writer can't get into a fight like this... he's grateful that guy stood up for him—thank you Frederic Forrest...Writer had a dream last night about his old best friend... Writer went to rehab and they weren't really friends anymore—artificial intelligence is becoming unwieldy and legitimately dangerous—an executive at Google quit his job today to talk more openly about this—every cliché science-fictional scenario is going to happen because people like Elon Musk and Jeff Bezos are incapable of living in a manner wherein they're not Smaug... that's probably Writer's fault... Writer's listening to an interview with the writer David Foster Wallace, done in San Francisco... in 2004, Wallace did some things in his life that are bad... he realized lately that you have to look within yourself in these situations and decide for yourself...

Writer would listen to someone talk to him who was a murderer... Writer would read a book by a murderer... Writer doesn't think doing something horrible ruins your chances of ever being able to write or communicate effectively or interestingly... this is just Writer's position on the matter... Writer understands other positions on the matter... a white guy behaving badly... Writer gets how this is a stupid thing to even have to think about… this has been a way of processing things, Writer thinks… Writer needed more money… Writer doesn't have enough money… he's so broke—Writer doesn't get paid too well to teach… he's trying to make do… his father died and Writer received some life insurance money from his passing—his father isn't dead… if Writer hadn't received that Writer couldn't just be teaching—did he quit the gas station… he'd need to work somewhere else… two places—or one place, that paid more… Writer doesn't know what to do or say… he's trying to figure out what Writer should say… Writer brought two unpeeled bananas with him into his car this morning because Writer didn't want to have to throw the peels someplace… Writer remembers eating one but Writer doesn't remember starting the second one… Writer hasn't found it… Writer doesn't know where it is… Writer fashioned an eyeglass ogle… a wonderful morning within the shitplanet—absence of shitplanet… no no—good planet…

The highest point at which human life and art meet is in the ordinary. To look down on the ordinary is to despise what you can't have. Show me a man who fears being ordinary, and I'll show you a man who is not yet a man. (Mishima)

Writer's taken his bath… Writer's washed behind his eyes… Writer, a skull… Writer can't wait for football season to end… thank god for basketball… Writer hates to see the sports… *give me a bit more gum with my steak*… hello and welcome to this Fuddruckers there are many others like it but this one is yours… join the military so as to shoot yourself more effectively in the forehead… yes yes—O good, another gun… Writer was worried there wouldn't be enough guns… another Perrier, sure… Writer meets D. for an anxious conversation at Starbucks, or Einstein's—or home—no no… *I'm not sure about these apostrophes*… Writer told me what—Writer said we needed to talk… Writer liked his time in graduate school—no no… Writer got to write about Darby Larson—he's still one of Writer's favorite writers… no no—Writer wonders what he's doing lately… Writer sits in the atrium with a bunch of candy… Writer teaches and a student takes over the class and he's relieved… Writer, bereaves… a little spot upon the ground where Writer has buried his father—no, the dog… no no—Writer's in the mud of it now… OK—his hands and feet are in the mud of it now… OK—the basketball courts… the mud hike—a rap battle as a teenager is a great source of pride… where did Writer hide all the stupid shit he's done… it's in the work—it's there—good… Matt Berninger singing "England" in the rain somewhere and his sister Chlöe tells him all about it—no no—she texts him… she's worried about him when she finds out Whitney Houston has died… Pusha T using that image of her bathroom sink on the cover of *Daytona* remains Writer's favorite artistic gesture of the twenty-first century… Writer would take that over all of Damien Hirst—OK… Writer would take that over the banana… Writer would take that over *My*

Struggle… it's the perfect artwork… it's the sequel to *American Psycho* we've all wanted so desperately in our complete disinterest as to whether a sequel like that would ever happen… *what the fuck is this guy talking about*… don't worry about how much gas a fuckin' car has… it can run on pure hardcore adrenaline… Writer likes to watch the video performances of Oka Takeshi on YouTube… Matthew Roberson said once that YouTube had taken over for TV—it's true… and Writer loves TV… Oka Takeshi or Takeshi Oka will play covers of lots of good songs on a guitar… Writer finds them moving to witness… Writer finds them highly comestible… Writer likes to sit there and imagine that his life could be like that… Writer doesn't want to write any new songs… Writer is content to try to learn to play part of these other songs, like the video…

dreamerika!

pay attention or don't—give your attention to something or do not… Writer might possibly—probably have a job—OK… the gas station—the university—it's a job and it isn't… it's your life—Writer wonders if L.R.D. worked, and where—what they did… William S. Burroughs got a large allowance until the day he died—explains a lot… L.R.D. worked—did he work—did he work in a shop—some shop… nobody knows—nobody cares—that's the downside… probably Writer can't make a living doing this—being this way… you would hope—you'd definitely hope for that… he's so grateful to be able to watch them… people say the world is in the worst shape it's ever been in… that hasn't been Writer's experience of things… people love to talk—geniuses love to talk, they're always talking—they love to slackline—they love being little pieces of shit… show us a genius and we'll show you a dead body—show me a Nobel Prize Winner and I'll show you Epstein's plane manifest… show us a genius and then get the fuck out of this apartment… show us—Writer bought what—Writer, buy the bleached shorts… no no—Writer can't wait for them to arrive… what's his UK size? Writer has no idea… how would Writer know that… how could Writer possibly know that… what Writer leaves you here with is his corpse… Writer's got a little bit of corpse left over from the leather jacket performance… *Leather Jacket* is a good band name a good name for this book a good name for the corpse performance… our corpse, who art in corpse, por favor his corpse cut his heart from his body to feed the lobby…

oh for fuck's sake—oh for fuck sake—oh for fucks sake—oh for crying in the beer… *they leave me at the restaurant*—Writer gets homesick kinda bad… can't help him—Writer's such a pussy—he's such a phony, a coward… he's such the worst for wear—he's worse for wear—he's worst for wear… Guy Davenport your malicious little face… goodnight Irene—cleanup on aisle five… Leadbelly killed somebody—did Leadbelly kill somebody… Woody Guthrie is someone—a dumb guitar… great an Irwin another dumb guitar—no no—the very best—Irwin the greatest guitars ever made, broke, homeless, when… Writer would've told himself to do away with the little limb or system in which Writer tried—tried—to fabricate a self… Writer would've been failing there—a failure there—and there—and there… Writer would've been at the salon—Writer would've been within the room and defecating—*my body would've been shitting there*… gross—a wonderful opportunity there—gross—to be shitting there… just so grateful Writer was attacked—just so grateful Writer got pummeled… Writer doesn't know himself much really now anymore… interested in the worst you've got… gimme the worst you've got… Writer can't wait to ingest the worst you've got… another documentary about a home—another bone—a body through which to burn oneself… a bathroom in which to work for Mister Nobody… his name spelled out like that—sure—the government narc—no no—who did it—who did that—who told on Nobody… wonderful, just fantastic—how long has Writer got to think it over… wet brain—the new world—divine inversion—the body of Christ pulled down from the cross… he's got another meeting in twenty-five minutes—another committee… he's so excited for it now… he's got some work to do—Dear Mister Oppenheimer… hello—hello and hello—Writer, defecating then—his body is there within the bathroom there… Writer has a great regret—Writer did a thing that Writer regrets… Writer doesn't know how to move forward from this thing—Writer wishes Writer knew but Writer does not know how to move forward from this thing… knowing this thing about the self… Writer doesn't know exactly what it was but he's afraid Writer hurt a person… no no—not physically—just the mental turmoil of the twenty-first century—no…

Forming grammatically correct sentences is for the normal individual the prerequisite for any submission to social laws. No one is supposed to be ignorant of grammaticality; those who are belong in special institutions. The unity of language is fundamentally political. (Deleuze)

just, you know—whatever else… people everywhere were starting to talk on the internet about following Christ… people you wouldn't expect—people everywhere… Writer wasn't a great person—sure, sure—yes… how is a person supposed to go forward from anything, from a bad thing, from anything good… Writer was realizing that from William S. Burroughs recently… Writer thought, fuck that guy—Joan Vollmer—Joan Vollmer Joan Vollmer…

Burroughs said he'd never have become a writer were it not for his accidental shooting of his wife Joan Vollmer… no no—Writer thought, fuck that guy… Writer didn't want to think about it, to hear about it… then recently Writer realized how special it made writing… writing could give you the apparatus with which to deal with having accidentally murdered your wife… or possibly it wasn't accidental—two people know, and they're both dead—it was horrible… did Writer already say this somewhere—somewhere else… or another manuscript—what is this manuscript—Writer might've—not sure… it's powerful, though, this notion—it helps him to empathize with him and with her more… writing gave this person in this awful situation that's entirely impossible to process a way of processing it… that's incredibly powerful—barring the potential reality that Burroughs was an actual psycho- or sociopath, which is obviously possible and perhaps even probable… Writer didn't shoot anybody, accidentally or otherwise… Writer didn't murder, didn't murder anybody… he's done things Writer doesn't feel good about but Writer knows that at least… and what of Christ, or of doubt—so maybe Writer can write—no no… maybe writing can continue to help Writer—maybe that's good… maybe Writer doesn't even need to publish it, or if Writer does, maybe Writer doesn't need to be afraid of the world anymore… of what—of the world—of the world, maybe… it's about the CIA… it's about this misconception that the CIA funded artwork during the Cold War… this isn't the thing people thought it was, Writer thought… people think that Jackson Pollock was pulled into CIA offices and told how to paint, Writer thought… really all it was was the CIA giving money to places that supported the arts—to try and highlight American art in the face of funding being given by the government to Russian art… if you think of it, Writer thought, this was actually amazing… try getting money for anything, ever… try getting money as a contemporary artist— nothing doing… try getting support for your book about the rainforest—nothing doing…

at one time in history the CIA gave money to artists, and we don't want to think about the world as it is, so we assume it's some conspiracy… people are so stupid, and most of all me, and most of all Writer… someone else said something about MFA programs—*go fuck yourself*—sure—people will do what they can do… if someone does something, we shouldn't just assume they're naïve idiots who don't want to put the real work in—*stop talking*… yes, sure, it's just that everybody isn't quite as smart as you… Writer saw the piece in the New Yorker— the piece in the New Yorker—the piece in the New Yorker—really compelling stuff… let's just assume that some mother who quit her job to get an MFA is a giant idiot and doesn't want to put the real work in… *do you really actually look at the things you write*… do you understand anything that doesn't happen on the American coasts… do you even care to… do you understand anything that doesn't happen in New York City… do you even care to…

yes I'm sure it's just the CIA and nobody is as smart as you… and book critics—don't get Writer started on book critics… the famous ones, Writer means—the ones who make money from it—these people who can't be bothered to look at a book that doesn't have a massive promotional budget and campaign behind it… *you're the fucking critics*… it's your job to explore the art in the world—the *world*, not New York City—not Twitter… *ohmygodshutthefuckup*… and you can't be bothered to read anything without a—the writers, the real writers, are lucky to make a couple hundred dollars a year—and the critics can't be bothered to do anybody a kindness—it's just too much—Writer hopes—Writer hopes the money is good…

To become imperceptible oneself, to have dismantled love in order to become capable of loving. To have dismantled one's self in order finally to be alone and meet the true double at the other end of the line. A clandestine passenger on a motionless voyage. To become like everybody else; but this, precisely, is a becoming only for one who knows how to be nobody, to no longer be anybody. To paint oneself gray on gray. (D & G)

I am beginning to wonder if my long habit of life amongst the insane is beginning to tell upon my own brain… buy some cigarettes—*wow can't handle how cool you are*… O wow smoking a cigarette it's so impressive—it's too impressive—get a life… peruse this paper—Writer's language would've had to be the thing… no no—every fuckup—every mistake… a klansman burning in the forest—burn the klansman in the forest—burn the forest ground—burn the woods—burn the lights—an idea for a boy… an idea for a sense of things where they now are upon the ground… a bottle filled with smaller cans of unsweetened green tea… he's drinking green tea again—he's drinking dieter's tea—it's having an effect on his brain… it's having an effect on his body—his body there within the room upon the ground—a little light… a nice morning in the hills of Europe—swimming in the water in the sun, with your friend the drunk—and a sense of alcoholism not really existing then… a body thusly upon the ground—his fandom for the old loser's Instagram—there, Writer presents himself… there his life is shone—no—shown—it is thus—it is shone… it is the light shone upon his life shown… Writer is within the classroom at the university with his body there pathetic there… hello and yes, Writer says it now and Writer wakes up in the morning and Writer talks to his wife about her work working on the TV show she's writing the TV show it's a beautiful thing to witness and Writer will check the mail eventually… walking within America in the small quiet town listening to *The OZ Tapes* it's clear and more recent wave of bands have missed a step concerning the notion of heaviness… heaviness, like lightness, is proportional, dependent upon circumstance, like gravity, or the density of the liquid you find yourself drowning in… what L.R.D. and L.R.D. figured out were the pocks in the wall of sound, the slow build of moments between sung lyrics, screeching soloing guitar—and simpler basslines that sound like they're being performed in the bar in *Twin Peaks*... heaviness when it's done thusly is a near constant state of transcendence, a vulnerability that doesn't stop with the performers—but extends to the listener and audience in a beautiful cohabitation and trust... they achieved what the Grateful Dead aspired to in their thousands of gigs—but did so in this removed manner, one that skipped over every accepted component of what a band could be... there is no band... there are no performers... there is no performance... what Writer finds so beautiful is it's there, it doesn't need to be spoken and we don't need to be pushed to it—it's right there... the release of *The OZ Tapes* could've ruptured music, the same way the sneaky publication of the Marquis de Sade could've halved Paris and the western world... but they didn't, and Writer thinks it's perhaps because they didn't want to—they didn't care, because, well, who gives a shit... they needed some version of the work to be put into the world, conveyed, and whatever happened after that couldn't have mattered any less—because they were already living out the promise of the work—the loud, transcending reaching of an artist living and showing the way to the hunched record collector—or the quasi-pervert flipping through Lautréamont at the university library...

But the impression becomes still stronger, if, when we have before our eyes, on a large scale, the battle of the raging elements, in such a scene we are prevented from hearing the sound of our own voice by the noise of a falling stream; or, if we are abroad in the storm of tempestuous seas, where the mountainous waves rise and fall, dash themselves furiously against steep cliffs, and toss their spray high into the air; the storm howls, the sea boils, the lightning flashes from black clouds, and the peals of thunder drown the voice of storm and sea. Then, in the undismayed beholder, the two-fold nature of his consciousness reaches the highest degree of distinctness. He perceives himself, on the one hand, as an individual, as the frail phenomenon of will, which the slightest touch of these forces can utterly destroy, helpless against powerful nature, dependent, the victim of chance, a vanishing nothing in the presence of stupendous might; and, on the other hand, as the eternal, peaceful, knowing subject, the condition of the object, and, therefore, the supporter of this whole world; the terrific strife of nature only his idea; the subject itself free and apart from all desires and necessities, in the quiet comprehension of the Ideas. This is the complete impression of the sublime. Here he obtains a glimpse of a power beyond all comparison superior to the individual, threatening it with annihilation. (Schopenhauer)

so, knowing this—or feeling this—or even just barely sensing this, it becomes a problem to try and write out the experience of a band, without writing their biography, and without aspiring to draw out in language the trajectory of the band's work, because Writer doesn't feel interested in that… Writer saves picture after picture of members of the band… Writer looks at them on his phone… Writer walked out one night, taking the dog for a piss, and listened to Flower Travellin' Band, and felt good... Writer reads interviews... Writer reads about sleuths trying to find L.R.D. or members of the group... Writer reads about Boredoms... Writer reads about Boris... Writer reads about violence and the Red Army Faction... *Ashita no Joe* being the hijackers and the bassist and their presence and Mishima's fondness for the manga... what are we to make of a mythology surrounding something? *White Light/White Heat* in the headphones of a student at a university somewhere in Japan... or in America, or in Peru—and this noise being interpreted in its way—in this way—and becoming something entirely different—entirely other... Writer can only hope to express what's drawn him to the sound, this feeling of burrowing inward and finding something representative there... a self, maybe... having no idea of the lyrics—no—a fan, maybe... having only the titles and various bits of script tied to their work... a shadow on our—their—joy... a body being pushed into something with the sound... lying down on your bed and welcoming this abrasive feedback—and beautiful guitars—a high moan over the whole of it as you play the *'77 Live* recording again, and this feeling that you might not even be listening to the band you're intending to listen to... the uncertainty—the surprise that came from realizing Jerry Garcia's heroin addiction—the chemical—the drug—the sadness at the passing of DJ Screw... the worlds these figures enacted in their work—because it's worlds—these aren't songs—each noise possesses a pitch, at times even a chord dominating over the whole of these irregular vibrations… these aren't albums… these are weeks—months—years of your life… there's no real rise or fall—but only within—only worlds—the slipstream of the work—this work—allowing people to bask in the warm water of another living… not a hand to hold so much as a hand in the center of your back and pushed through to the center into your solar plexus as you begin to fall from the balcony of some party somewhere anywhere and everybody's soaking wet… you're held—but only just—and if you writhe from it your spine could break—your ribs could protrude out and your place within the world would be as a void… the art of noises must not be limited to a mere imitative reproduction… someone wants to understand the context in which this stuff is being released… someone wants to read the diaries of who made this material… Writer views the material as the diary—the only thing we'll need… so they are students, they are leftists, they are fascists, they are violent, they are peaceful, they worship death, they are the poisoning on the train, Giacinto Scelsi's recording being randomly linked to that on the internet somewhere—and nobody really knowing why it should be that way—no no— nobody knowing the motivation for connecting these two figures… and that's alright—because again—we might not even be listening to the band, or we might be listening to something that the band, or L.R.D. would be furious to comprehend… a thing stolen— the work never being yours… the pact you've entered into in this situation… the agreement that the best you can get won't even come close… you'd need to be there—you'd need to be in the room… you'd need to be there in the basement of the record shop where they're performing… you'd need to be there as they played with other groups and recordings were made and there were two guitars and one bass and no drums and they moaned high up in that whiny manner that coats the tops of the guitar sounds as he stands there with his large guitar plucking solo notes idly above the chords being strummed by the woman—and the bassist, and things are peaceful…

the band performing at a ski resort—as part of a festival… and was it just mythology that the organizers of the event asked the band to turn it down for fear of an avalanche? and was it just mythology that the band kept playing, and everybody scattered in fear? you can see a version of the recording… Writer thinks so, anyway—Writer doesn't know who talks to whom and Writer doesn't know what really to make of any of it, much like Writer doesn't know much of anything at all when it comes to trying to explain anything ever… they are a corpus—a body—they are there upon the stage in the—on the stage or in the moody room wherein they're playing a long and ambling set… how could anybody ever know anything at all…

RE/SEARCH; or, More Notes Toward the Definition of Culture "Official Releases" via lesrrallizesdenudes-official.com/discography『THE OZ TAPES』レーベル：Temporal Drift（DRFT03）2x LPリリース：2022年4月27日 Side A　1. OZ Days　2. A Shadow on Our Joy / 僕ら

の喜びに影がさした　3. Wilderness of False Flowers / 造花の原野　4. White Awakening / 白い目覚めSide B　1. The Last One_1970Side C　1. Memory is Far Away / 記憶は遠い　2. Vertigo Otherwise My Conviction / 眩暈Side D1.　The Last One_1970 (ver.2)『'67-'69 Studio et Live』Rivista Inc. – SIXE-0101リリース：1991年8月15日（out of print）Smokin' Cigarette Blues (Live Version)La Mal Rouge眩暈 otherwise My Conviction-Les Bulles de Savon記憶は遠い鳥の声My Conviction (2nd Version)The Last OneWriter(Live Version)『Mizutani / Les Rallizes Dénudés』Rivista Inc. – SIXE-0203リリース：1991年8月15日（out of print）記憶は遠い朝の光 L'AUBE断章 I断章 II亀裂THE LAST ONE黒い悲しみのロマンセ otherwiseFallin'Love With『'77Live』（2CD）Rivista Inc. – SIXE-0400リリース：1991年8月15日（out of print）Disque 1Enter the Mirror夜、暗殺者の夜氷の炎記憶は遠いDisque 2夜より深く夜の収穫者たちThe Last One『Les Rallizes Dénudés』(VHS)リリース：1992年9月15日（out of print）収録曲氷の炎夜、暗殺者の夜THE LAST ONE　他「Les Rallizes Dénudés」(雑誌『etcetera　vol.2』付録)リリース：1996年9月（out of print）収録曲A　黒い悲しみのロマンセ或いはFallin' Love WithB　永遠に今が『OZ DAYS LIVE』（2枚組コンピレーションLP・裸のラリーズはD面のみ収録）OZ Records – OZ-1, OZ-2リリース：1973年8月（out of print）収録曲SIDE-A（都おち/アシッド セブン）Part 1Part 2Part 3Part 4Part 5Part 6SIDE-B（南正人）Part 1Part 2Part 3Part 4SIDE-C（タジマハール旅行団）Part　1SIDE-D（裸のラリーズ）

Part 1Part 2Part 3Part 4Bootleg releases via WikipediaBlind Baby Has Its Mother's EyesCable Hogue SoundtrackDouble HeadsFrance Demo TapeGreat White WonderHeavier Than a Death in the FamilyMars Studio 1980Flightless Bird Needs Water Wings (溺れる飛べない鳥は水羽が必要, Oboreru tobenaitori wa Mizuha ga hitsuyō)Yodo-Go-A-Go-Go

it is simple—the thing—the thing you need to put down is simple… it is simple, Writer, the thing you wish to state is simple—the words, they're simple—we promise you… you are trying to express something that people have been trying to express for a long time and when it comes right down to it it's very simple… the thing that isn't simple is your life—which presents problems—there, right there… life is not simple… expression is simple enough… or at root perhaps it's simple—or perhaps it's supposed to be simple… perhaps it isn't even simple… perhaps it's not simple… the thing is it isn't like a scream… or maybe it's like a scream but not a scream that stops… we think of the scream as having a stop… we think of a band's performance ending… maybe it's not so simple—or maybe it's not only life—or maybe it's not just life but it's other things too, or maybe the thing remains pretty simple but to do it in a way that's admirable is not simple… it's not enough to just scream—no no… if it were enough to just scream then people wouldn't get divorces or kill themselves… the overworked manager in her office screaming into a pillow—that isn't enough… so they scream in the car, too… then they go home to their spouse and they quiet down, and they fester, and it's back to work in the morning—back to work, back to work—or it's tending to their children, or it's whatever else… so it becomes this complicated thing—this desire to scream, but the scream not being enough… after that what does a person have—life—living—the world—the entire world of people, and work, and marriage, and money, and debt, and anger, and all of it… and it's simple—and it's not simple—and it's everywhere, and you're surrounded… the fundament, though—the fundament of the person doing something in reaction to the stupidity of living, and the stupidity of life—and the stupidity of their existence, and every infuriating element of it—sure, fine—accept it…

This quality of concepts by which they resemble the stones of a mosaic, and on account of which perception always remains their asymptote, is also the reason why nothing good is produced in art by their means. If the singer or the virtuoso attempts to guide his execution by reflection he remains silent. And this is equally true of the composer, the painter, and the poet. The concept always remains unfruitful in art; it can only direct the technical part of it, its sphere is science. We shall consider more fully in the third book, why all true art proceeds from sensuous knowledge, never from the concept. Indeed, with regard to behaviour also, and personal agreeableness in society, the concept has only a negative value in restraining the grosser manifestations of egotism and brutality; so that a polished manner is its commendable production. But all that is attractive, gracious, charming in behaviour, all affectionateness and friendliness, must not proceed from the concepts, for if it does, "we feel intention, and are put out of tune." All dissimulation is the work of reflection; but it cannot be maintained constantly and without interruption: "nemo potest personam diu ferre fictum," says Seneca in his book de clementia; and so it is generally found out and loses its effect. Reason is needed in the full stress of life, where quick conclusions, bold action, rapid and sure comprehension are required, but it may easily spoil all if it gains the upper hand, and by perplexing hinders the intuitive, direct discovery, and grasp of the right by simple understanding, and thus induces irresolution. (Schopenhauer)

Writer doesn't know what to make of the notion of God—no no... some days Writer feels as though all Writer wants to do is be entirely consumed by a religiousness... some days Writer feels violently angry at God... Writer doesn't know why there's this curiosity towards Catholicism... it's everywhere in writing—it's everywhere on the internet... the tradcath—*jesuschristcutmyheadoff*... Dostoevsky is a kind of god, or an intermediary—Dostoevsky would be Writer's god... Dostoevsky is God... Writer in the hotel room late thinking about James Joyce could be his god, and that would be sufficient, and then falling finally to sleep—James Joyce is Writer's god... if only Writer had the patience to read it all— read everything... the band seems opposed to the notion—to a notion of good, though maybe that's just a limited view... amplifier worship—amplifier sickness—amplifier nausea... a guitar as a device with which you can tap into pure desire or purer expression of a representation of the will—we need an instrument, to take a measurement... Writer doesn't know—as a father Writer doesn't know—no, no... as a husband Writer doesn't know... Writer wants to be good at these things—AA, Writer guessed, is a god for people like him... the people there... the people there dying there and talking there... nobody there being any better or any worse off at any given time... no no... the people in their living there... who is Writer to talk this way? L.R.D., Writer guessed, is a god for him... mumble into the microphone... Writer has a CD of *Heavier Than a Death in the Family* in his car... he'd put it on and let it wash over him—which Writer thought was the best way to experience the band... perhaps any band...

Writer doesn't know if God exists but Writer knows it isn't him... is that the extent of it? is that what matters? hit your knees—*you sound like a cop*—kneel down—prayer being the things you say in such a position... strap the guitar to your body... kneel down upon the ground—plug in—touch the head of your guitar to the amplifier... the direction of the band was determined the minute my electric guitar fed back... fed back—feedback—feedbacker—fangs anal satan... Writer got a tattoo across his gut reading LUCIFER, a few months after his daughter was born, his first child—*who gives a shit*... Writer was learning to accept the new life before him... still learning—amor fati... Writer was taking it in...

Writer was learning to accept the life before him… Writer said, Writer has a child, but Writer doesn't want to become the kind of person who wouldn't have LUCIFER tattooed across his gut… Writer liked Kenneth Anger… Writer liked more the Milton notion of Lucifer as a kind of beaten-down loser, a human expression of pushing back… time to time Writer does feel shame having it on his gut—when Writer goes swimming with his family, say, he'll feel embarrassed… not enough, though, as it does seem to force him to think seriously about the notion of god and the notion of the devil… L.R.D. is dead… long live L.R.D.… L.R.D. died two years ago—their website confirmed it… what did it say—their former band mate was working with a family who inherited L.R.D.'s recordings to put these things out—OK… the website and the *OZ Tapes* their first output in any capacity in a very long time… their first message in a very long time… also, L.R.D. was already dead—however long… what tragedy, what a horrible thought… such a life—such is life—people die—and maybe there's some kind of god… *I'll pray to the people in those meetings*—no no… although part of him winces when typing L.R.D. instead of whatever, this would seem to be a benefit of becoming a fan of a band that could care less about him and whatever Writer might get from their music… to some extent, the shortening seems like an endearment, like Writer wants quicker access to their work, like he'd want to carve it into every table Writer ever sits at… what came first, Rich Kids on LSD or RKL? Public Image Ltd. or PiL? does it matter? of course it matters!

it doesn't... do you know how best to proceed? of course not! the point is the referring... to become a member of the legion of this thing—OK... the naked members of Flower Travellin' Band upon their motorcycles... Boris, Wata, Takeshi, Atsuo—playing a club in Japan where a skinny white American and a young Japanese man become the best of friends in the audience—sure—raising up their skinny wrists in connection with this abrasive scraping gesture they're trapped in together... trapped there—Writer is not American person who is good... OK—he's not a good American upon a plane... Writer is not within the CIA going to Japan to root out the leftists—OK... Writer is not an American leftist—Writer is not an American conservative... Writer is a body on the American step... Writer is not the American upon the orchard's floor... Writer is not a good and righteous American upon the orchard's floor... Writer is not an American upon the jet—no no... Writer is not an American—Writer is not the redesigned airport there... Writer is not the good and righteous American there... Writer is not an American upon the dirt there under the dirt below there... Writer is not Frederick Exley weeping in the room—nor John Fante and the oranges—nor Céline and the cats, the dogs... Writer is not Frederick Exley's manuscript for *Mean Greenwich Time*... Writer is not Richard Stark or some other American person...

Writer is not a good body of the American of the blood on the dining room floor or Yukio the fascist or Gertrude Stein the fascist... Writer is a bad avant pop—a prop... no no... Writer goes for walks by the fields within Washington within America... Writer is not there within America... Writer is not upon the jet Writer is within the French apartment with L.R.D.—Writer does not want to enjoy this in retrospect Writer wants to be a person who enjoys something in living now, today, now—no no... Writer is not an American on the floor there of the plane there that's being taken as it's gassed up... Writer is hiding in the Tokyo apartment reading *Nausea*, no, reading *Being and Nothingness*, no, reading *A Thousand Plateaus*—no reading...

perhaps everything would've been better if he'd done everything in a completely different way from the beginning of his life writing... perhaps people aren't meant to do this kind of thing—bootlegs—bootlegs hidden everywhere hiding... perhaps they're hidden everywhere hiding and Writer's trying to think about if this were the case for some writer—no willful releases—nothing willfully released... except at the end, after his death... do you exist? if a band doesn't release an album but an album of that band is released, does it make a sound? does a bootleg make a sound? does a person make a sound when they leave this world? those odd little breaths... his dog made those odd little breaths when it died... Writer saw a TV show where a dog ate drugs and lived... Writer called the vet the night his dog ate some pills and it had ripped into them and told the vet had eaten these drugs, and the vet was an old man and didn't seem to know what to do, and indicated the typical things they tell you online about getting it to puke… it had been too long at that point… the drugs were in its system… had it been too long… in the morning the dog died… he's written about this before… Writer doesn't know where Writer wrote about this before… perhaps he's always repeating things—he's paranoid… the same old stories—nothing… Writer doesn't know what he's supposed to do about this… Writer doesn't know what a writer is supposed to do about anything… Writer doesn't think a person can do very much… Writer doesn't think a person can do very much in their living… we have been led to believe we can do more than we can do and Writer thinks we should resign ourselves to the warming reality that we can't do very much… it's a miracle that we even live… stop trying to fix everything… stop trying to fix everyone… people are people—people are what they are—the world is filled with flaws… the world of man is filled with flaws—it's alright—being alive is alright—being a person alive is alright… being an American is alright… everything is fine—the things that aren't fine might need rectifying—that's fine—let's rectify them if we can… but if we cannot—that's alright… Writer used to get very mad at people who didn't vote, say… Writer used to get very mad, sure… then things kept happening—living kept happening—and now Writer can understand… Writer understands a person not wanting to vote… Writer understands people who don't get invested in things… Writer understands people who just want to live the way they want to live… Writer thinks that's a noble pursuit… Writer thinks it's a noble thing to do something because you want to do it—or because you feel it's right—or something—no no… people are always trying to fix things—fix everything… people are always putting their noses into the business of other people… people never leave people alone… people never just leave people alone and quiet down… possibly though that's the only thing we can really do—anybody, anybody… and maybe that's fine— maybe that is—maybe it is… Writer doesn't want to say anymore definitely that any one thing is a thing, or the thing… Writer doesn't want to talk that way anymore… Writer doesn't care about that, about knowing… Writer doesn't care about a lot of things… we've been led to believe that caring about a lot of things is a thing, perhaps the only thing… we think things—things think themselves—things think things thinking things…

good riddance—a small hand upon your back… a rabbit putting its paw on yours—a lucky foot… a good piece of music—a bad piece of music… sitting in a room in California where you're crying like a little baby… sitting in a hot room in California with a tape you were sent in the mail by someone at a university in Tokyo—OK… sitting in a hot room typing something while the tape plays and you try to imagine yourself at the venue, at the show—and putting your hands on the stage and your hands being stepped on—as you type, writing—gently, by the singer of the band… cancer as a social activity… and this would be a beautiful life for you… a pathetic, stupid, beautiful life for you… and you're sitting down there on the edge of the state there reading a book written by a dictator about film and trying to understand how things got this way… sitting in a room in California and your kids are in the next room—and you've been fired from your job—and your wife is at the laundromat—and tomorrow you will go to the track and place bets and drink coffee and sit in the sun and bask in all that life has given you… and maybe now you're getting older— and maybe now you're diabetic… and maybe now it's a very cold day—lonely, on Bunker Hill… and maybe now it's winter and you are writhing on the floor in pain—and you'd like to be outside, two in the morning, meditating under a large snowy pine tree—and maybe now you can't see anymore— maybe you've had a stroke, the diary finished, the work on your porch sitting, waiting—and maybe now your wife will have to take dictation of your work, this final work… and you will narrate your last book—and then you will die—surrounded by your family—in a hot room in California… with a tape on the shelf that you used to listen to while you worked—while you wept—and everything will be peaceful—and the world will know peace—and God will smile down on you and tell you that you are a child again—that you have worked to deserve this kind of thing, this state—and your wife will play you this song, Writer—and it will resonate with you, and burrow into you, and it will creep into your blood… and you will feel calmed by the good work of another human being—another group of human beings—or the hand of your wife on yours—in the sun, in the sun… those who got together—those who got an instrument—those who said we need this, and we haven't the faintest idea why—to see something—to figure something out… and they will do so—and your body will be buried in a cemetery surrounded by the other dead—and it will be a warm day in California in the light—and you will not need to speak…

Grant Maierhofer is the author of *Shame*, *Peripatet*, *The Compleat Lungfish*, and others. He lives in Moscow, Idaho.

PUBLISHED BY ERRATUM REPRINTS

The Scourge of Villanie
John Marston

Civilisation Its Cause and Cure
Edward Carpenter